TRAPPED IN THE PANHANDLE

Tucker McCall—Skilled in survival on the Western plains, he had to choose between his boss's cold cash and his growing love for an Eastern woman.

Lacey Ellis—She had come to Texas with her fiancé from Boston, but the harsh, unforgiving Panhandle taught her a lesson in living and loving she would never forget.

Burl Wayne—With the buffalo herds dying out, one last hunt would make him rich, and he didn't much care how many buffalo—or people—were killed.

Allen Kerry—A tenderfoot banker from the East, he was caught in a crossfire of violence, and the only man who could get him out alive was his rival for Lacey Ellis.

Helen Wayne—She had lived a life of degradation, but now she had hope—if she didn't die from an arrow or from Burl Wayne's bullet.

The Stagecoach Series
Ask your bookseller for the books you have missed

STAGECOACH STATION 29:
PANHANDLE

Hank Mitchum

Created by the producers of
Wagons West, White Indian, and
Saga of the Southwest.

Chairman of the Board: Lyle Kenyon Engel

BANTAM BOOKS
TORONTO • NEW YORK • LONDON • SYDNEY • AUCKLAND

STAGECOACH STATION 29: PANHANDLE
A Bantam Book / May 1987

Produced by Book Creations, Inc.
Lyle Kenyon Engel, Founder

ISBN 0-553-26467-2

Published simultaneously in the United States and Canada

PRINTED IN THE UNITED STATES OF AMERICA

O   0 9 8 7 6 5 4 3 2 1

STAGECOACH STATION 29:

PANHANDLE

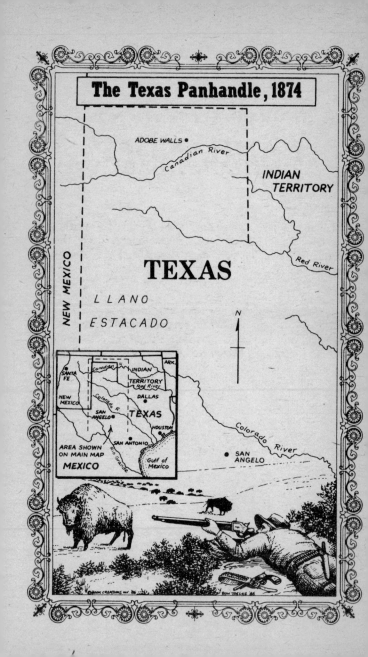

The Texas Panhandle, 1874

Chapter One

It was a typical spring day in the Texas Panhandle in the year 1874—the sky was gray and overcast, the thick clouds occasionally splitting to dump hard rain showers on the plains. Here, just south of the border between Texas and the Indian Territory, most of the vegetation was still brown from the previous winter, but as the weather warmed and the rains continued, it would begin to turn green. And then summer would arrive with its blistering heat and cloudless skies, and this whole region would turn brown and dusty again.

The rutted stagecoach trail leading south was not dusty at the moment. It was a roiling sea of mud that splashed up from the hooves of the six-horse team and sucked at the wheels of the Concord stagecoach making its way along the rough road. On the seat atop the driver's box, Ben Proctor huddled miserably in his slicker and kept up a steady stream of cursing as he whipped the animals on.

Proctor knew that if he let the coach slow, it might bog down in the mud. He was a veteran driver, middle-aged and grizzled, and pushing these rigs along was the thing he knew best.

Next to him, Willie Morse, the young shotgun guard, was just as wet and uncomfortable. Willie had his shotgun inside his slicker, trying to keep the rain from it. There was not much he could do about the steady trickle of water dripping down his neck from the floppy brim of his hat.

"Damned Texas weather," Proctor growled. "Hot in the summer and cold in the winter and rainin' the rest of the time." His voice trailed off in muttered invective.

"Reckon it could be worse," Willie answered, though at the moment he did not see how.

"And it could be a whole hell of a lot better," Proctor snapped. "We could be inside this here coach where it's dry."

"Wouldn't be anybody to drive it, then." Willie shivered in his slicker, a damp chill running through him. "We'd be stuck out here."

Proctor could not argue with that bit of logic, so he did not try. Instead, he contented himself with hurling more coarse words into the wind.

It was drier inside the coach, but that did not mean that the passengers were riding in the lap of luxury. The stage line was small, unable to afford new coaches, and this old Concord, though still structurally sound, had a few leaks in its roof. The canvas curtains that were drawn across the windows kept out some of the rain, but they billowed in with each gust of wind, letting in some of the downpour.

Lacey Ellis, who rode facing backward on the front seat, leaned back against the hard wood of the bench and moved her right leg so that the drops from a particularly persistent leak would not soak her dress. She glanced at the woman sitting beside her and tried to smile as she met the unhappy gaze of her future sister-in-law.

"It'll be all right, Eleanora," Lacey said, injecting a note of cheer in her voice. "I'm sure the rain won't last too much longer."

Eleanora Morrison sighed wearily. "Perhaps not, but I'm sure that when it ends, there will be something else equally unpleasant to beset us."

Lacey did not try to argue with her. If there was one thing she had learned on this long trip from Boston, it was that arguing with Eleanora was futile.

On the surface, there were similarities between the two women. Both were dressed in clothes purchased in Boston's finest dress shops, and both were attractive. At twenty-one, though, Lacey was a decade younger than Eleanora, and even under these conditions there was a fresh beauty about her. Her brunette hair was rich and lustrous despite the dampness. Her good looks were natural.

Eleanora's attractiveness, on the other hand, was the result of hard work and a carefully planned denial of her true age. The artisans of Boston's salons had done their work well, from the stylish hat perched atop her blond hair to the dainty slippers on her feet. At the moment, though, the ringlets of hair were drooping, and the shoes were spattered with mud from the coach's last stop. Eleanora looked as though she was doing her best not to cry.

Of all the places she could have been, Texas was the absolute worst, to her way of thinking.

Two men occupied the seat opposite Lacey and Eleanora, the center bench being empty. Allen Kerry was looking through the crack around the curtain covering the window beside him. He frowned at the gray day outside, determined not to be drawn into the discussion between Lacey, who was his fiancée, and Eleanora, his sister. Getting involved in a potential argument between the two women was the last thing he wanted.

Besides, he was too busy wondering just what he was doing here. He should have been back in Boston. It rained there, too, of course, but at least when it did, a civilized man could retreat to the warmth and comfort of a roaring fireplace and a glass of fine brandy.

Louis Shepherd, seated next to Allen Kerry, had never been to Boston. In fact, the farthest east he had ever been was Dallas. But at the moment, as he swayed back and forth with the bouncing motion of the stage, he would have appreciated some brandy every bit as much as his more cultured seatmate.

Hell, in weather like this, even a shot of rotgut whiskey would go down nice.

Shepherd told himself to stop thinking about whiskey. He had a flask in his case, but that was in the luggage boot. Besides, the shiny silver vessel was hidden underneath the Bibles he was hawking on this trip. He had been riding the stage with these people for three days, and he had created a solid image with them that he did not want to shatter.

Shepherd had plans for the pretty widow lady called Eleanora. He smiled at her, trying to convey his sincere sympathy with her discomfort.

In return, Eleanora forced a tiny smile onto her thinly compressed lips. Getting to know Louis Shepherd was the only good thing that had happened so far on this ill-conceived journey. When he had first boarded the coach in Dodge City three days before, he had introduced himself as a traveling salesman, but his sober dark suit and polite demeanor was a marked contrast to that of the flashy, drunken drummers who had shared their coach before.

Shepherd was a tall, lithe man in his thirties sporting a neatly trimmed dark beard. In unguarded moments, Eleanora found herself thinking he was one of the most handsome men she had ever seen—certainly more handsome than her late husband had ever been. It was not that she hadn't cared for her husband. But he had been considerably older—a business associate of her father's—and her widowhood at an early age was not unexpected.

Lacey saw the quick smile that passed between Eleanora and Shepherd, and she suppressed the urge to sigh and roll her eyes heavenward. Eleanora might have been taken in by the slick charm of the man, but Lacey knew better. She had seen his kind before.

But maybe she was being too suspicious, she thought. Shepherd might really be an itinerant Bible salesman, just as he claimed. At any rate, Eleanora's choice of friends was not any business of hers.

Lacey closed her eyes for a moment and tried to rest her head against the front wall of the coach. The ride was too rough for that, however, so she sat up and reached out to pull back the curtain next to her, hoping to spot a landmark that would tell her where they were. She moved the canvas only a bit, trying to keep out as much of the rain as possible. This journey to her father's ranch seemed to be taking forever. When she thought about her father, with his gruff manner and unexpected kindnesses, she felt a pang of anticipation.

It had been two years since her last visit to the great Rafter E ranch owned by her father, Sam Ellis, near San Angelo—two long years since she had put on jeans, mounted a horse, and ridden out to take part in the spring roundup. Sam Ellis had drawn the line at allowing her to accompany the herd as it was pushed north through Indian Territory to the railhead in Kansas. A trail drive was no place for a nineteen-year-old girl, according to Sam, and Lacey had to admit that he was probably right.

She did not have to like it, however, any more than she had to like the situation between her mother and father. Never had a more unlikely match been made than the one between Sam Ellis and Virginia Ashford. The daughter of an old, established Boston family, Virginia had viewed Sam as a dashing, romantic cowboy when she had met him during a tour of the West. The attraction between the two of them, coupled with a slight rebellious streak that made Virginia delight in shocking her parents, had led the young couple to get married.

Sam had naturally expected Virginia to remain with him on the ranch he was just establishing, and at first she had gone along with his wishes. But despite honestly loving Sam, Virginia had soon realized she could not spend the rest of her life in a land that she regarded as a wilderness. The rugged existence of Texas ranch life was simply too much for her.

Virginia left the Rafter E and returned to the bosom of her family in Boston, carrying within her the child that had turned out to be Lacey. Her family had welcomed her back, though they never entirely forgave her for marrying a man like Sam Ellis.

Lacey's earliest memory of her father was of a tall man with a sweeping mustache who wore strange clothes and carried a large hat. He had seemed ill at ease in the hushed rooms of the Ashford mansion, but he had come

east to see his daughter and would not leave until he
had done so.

"Lacey, this is your father," Virginia had told the
little girl. Shyly, Lacey had gone to him. He had stood
still at first, but then swept Lacey up into his arms and
fiercely hugged her to him.

For a moment, Lacey had been frightened, but
then somehow she had sensed the rightness of his embrace and knew that the tall man loved her with all his
heart. She snuggled against him, not bothering to wonder why her father had never visited before.

"Ginny, I want the girl to come visit me when
she's old enough," Sam Ellis said in a strangely choked
voice.

At the time, Lacey had been too young to notice
her mother's look of disapproval. If Virginia had her
way, Lacey would have nothing to do with Texas. Sam
was insistent, though, and when Lacey was eight years
old, she made the first of her trips west, accompanied
by a governess. Virginia wanted no part of Texas, not
even for a short trip.

As the years went by, Lacey continued to visit her
father, sometimes every summer for several years in a
row. She began to comprehend the strange situation
between her parents, who were still married though
they had not seen each other in over ten years. Her
mother and father still claimed to love each other, but
neither was willing to leave home to live with the other
one.

As for Lacey, she loved both of them dearly . . .
but she had to admit that she felt much more at home
now in Texas.

From the first time she had seen the ranch, seen
the rolling hills carpeted with lush grass, seen the huge
herds of cattle, seen the pride that her father took in
the spread he had built with his own hands, she had
fallen in love with the place. Sam Ellis was a busy man,
but when Lacey visited, he took the time to show her
every corner of the ranch and teach her about a life that
was totally different from what she had known back
east.

By the time she was twelve, she was as much at home on the back of a horse as she was in the ballroom of the mansion in Boston. She could handle a rope and shoot a rifle. Sam had taught her how to fire a Colt, though the recoil strained her wrist at first.

At the time of her last visit, when she was nineteen, she had come to an important decision: The next time she came to the ranch, she was going to stay. Texas was going to be her home.

Then she had returned to Boston, been introduced to Allen Kerry, and almost against her will found herself falling in love.

She looked at Allen now as he rode on the opposite seat of the bouncing coach, and a quick smile passed between them. He was, without a doubt, the best catch in Boston.

The son of a prominent banking family, Allen Kerry seemed to have every advantage a young man could want. He was handsome, with crisp, dark hair and blue eyes, and he was rich. All over the city, mothers had schemed to pair their daughters with him. He was in his midtwenties, a charming, highly eligible bachelor . . . until Lacey Ellis came along.

They had met at a party given by Allen's parents, and during their first conversation, Lacey had talked with him about things that interested her. Eventually, ignoring her mother's cautionary frown, she had told him about her father's ranch in Texas, and Allen seemed to hang on her description of it. Lacey had concluded by the end of the evening that Allen Kerry was an intelligent and self-confident young man.

Within a year, they were engaged to be married.

Lacey was not going to let her engagement stop her from making this trip to see her father, however. She had spent the last few months persuading Allen to come along with her. She wanted the two men who meant the most to her to meet. Sam Ellis, after all, would be Allen's father-in-law.

Allen had been hesitant at first, since the trip would keep him away from business for several weeks, but eventually he had agreed to accompany her to

Texas. But propriety demanded that someone else go along to act as chaperone, and when Allen's recently widowed sister, Eleanora, had insisted, the task had fallen to her.

Lacey had hoped Allen and Eleanora would enjoy the journey, but so far they had been bored and uncomfortable. Allen regretted his decision to come, Lacey was sure of that, and now this damned rain was making things worse.

As if responding to her thoughts, the pounding of the rain on the coach roof suddenly slackened and then gradually tapered off to nothing. Willie Morse leaned down from his seat on the box and called to the passengers, "Looks like we're finally out of the storm, folks."

"And none too soon," Eleanora commented sharply. "Really, I've never seen such unpleasant weather."

Lacey bit her tongue, suppressing the urge to remind the other woman of the miserable winters they had seen in Boston. From the look on his face, Allen shared his sister's relief at the end of the rain.

The clouds began to break up, letting several brilliant rays of sunlight slant down to the ground. Yet the light did little to dispel the chill in the air.

The trail became less muddy, though the ride was just as rough. Lacey was looking forward to stretching her legs at the next way station. She remembered from previous trips that it was a meal stop. Hot food would be more than welcome; it was now past noon, and none of the passengers had had anything to eat since breakfast, just after sunrise.

As the coach continued down the trail, none of its occupants noticed the two figures on horseback, watching from a small hill three-quarters of a mile away. After a few moments, the riders turned their unshod ponies and galloped away.

The stage pulled into the yard of the way station less than half an hour later. Ben Proctor hauled up on the team, and the coach rocked on its broad leather thoroughbraces as it came to a stop.

Proctor and Willie swung down from the box as hostlers came forward to begin the changing of the team. The station manager was waiting for them in the doorway of the low adobe building. He nodded a greeting to the driver and guard and asked, "Any trouble along the way, boys?"

"Not unless you count the damned rain," Proctor replied grumpily. "Hope your wife kept the grub hot for us, Riordan."

"She did," the station manager said. "I knew you'd be along. You wouldn't let a few Indians bother you, would you, Ben?"

Proctor and Willie looked sharply at Riordan, and then Proctor asked flatly, "Indians? They causin' trouble?"

The station manager shrugged. "Word has it that Quanah has been firing them up, him and that Quahadi war chief Bear Running. Could just be a bunch of talk, though."

"Anybody been hurt yet?" Willie asked.

Riordan hesitated and then said, "I heard that a little party of buffalo hunters was killed down close to the Canadian River. Don't say anything about it where the womenfolk can hear, boys."

"Sounds like more than a bunch of talk to me," Proctor said. "Wish somebody'd warned us back up the line some."

"What would you have done? Wouldn't you have come ahead anyway?"

Proctor smiled slightly, but there was no humor in it. "Reckon I would have," he said.

As Proctor, Willie, and Riordan talked in front of the doorway, Allen Kerry opened the door of the coach and stepped out, being careful where he put his feet. The yard of the station was muddy in places, though it obviously had not rained as much here. Allen turned around and reached out to help Lacey down from the stage, but Eleanora moved into the door first, so that Allen had to hand her down in front of Lacey. Louis Shepherd was the last one off the coach.

"My goodness," Eleanora said breathlessly, "I think I've forgotten what it feels like not to be bouncing around in that awful vehicle."

"We'll be stopped here for a little while," Lacey

told her. "The station manager's wife should have a meal ready for us."

"Something better than the fare at the last station, I hope," Allen said. "Allow me, ladies," he said as he linked arms with the two women, Lacey to his left and Eleanora to his right, and led them toward the station building.

Shepherd followed along behind, slightly annoyed with Allen. He had been intending to offer his arm to Eleanora. He knew quite well that she was interested in him, and it was time he started building on the relationship. He had originally planned to leave the stage before it reached San Angelo, but now he had decided to stay on board as long as Eleanora did. A liaison with such a woman could prove quite profitable for him in the long run.

Lacey noticed that Proctor, Willie, and the station manager fell silent as the passengers approached, but she did not see anything unusual in that. The station manager turned toward them and smiled. "Howdy, folks," he said. "Just go on in and make yourselves at home."

The three men stood aside to let the passengers go through the low door. Shepherd had to stoop slightly. Inside the building the air was even cooler than outside, the small fire in the fireplace doing little to cut the chill. Vegetation was sparse in this part of the country, and people had to make do with small fires of mesquite branches and dried buffalo chips.

In the center of the room was a sturdy, rough-hewn table upon which Riordan's wife, a stout woman in an apron and a simple cotton dress, was setting a steaming pot of stew. Bowls were already on the table, ready to be filled.

"Help yourselves," the woman grunted. Evidently she was not happy about the late arrival of the stagecoach.

Allen took his hat off and laid it on the table and then held a chair for Lacey. Seeing this, Shepherd moved in quickly, drawing out a chair and holding it for Eleanora. She gave him a wan smile and said, "Thank you, Mr. Shepherd. I'm glad someone in this wilderness knows how to behave graciously."

"We're not all unlettered barbarians out here, Mrs. Morrison," Shepherd replied as he took a seat across the table from her.

"I'm sure Eleanora meant no offense, Mr. Shepherd," Lacey said quickly when she saw that Eleanora was not going to temper her remark.

Shepherd waved a hand and smiled across the table at Eleanora. "No offense, I assure you. This part of the country *is* rather lacking in gracious behavior."

"I'm surprised to find a man like yourself out here, Shepherd," Allen said as he dished out a bowl of the greasy stew. He looked dubiously at the food, as if he was not sure what was in it but knew he did not want to ask. Then he passed it on to Lacey, who was sitting beside him.

Shepherd shrugged in response to Allen's comment. "I just go where my business takes me," he said. "I prefer New Orleans or St. Louis or Philadelphia, but at the present time . . ." He shrugged again.

Eleanora leaned forward, interest brightening her face. "Have you ever been to Boston, Mr. Shepherd?"

"I'm afraid not, though I'd enjoy visiting your lovely city sometime." Shepherd knew better than to lie. He could bluff his way so long as the conversation was about New Orleans or St. Louis; he had talked to enough people from those cities that he would not get caught in a major error. But he was not going to claim that he had been to Boston, not when his three companions had lived there for years.

Allen had his own bowl of stew now, and he was regarding it with uncertainty. He picked up a wooden spoon and took a tentative taste. It was better than it looked.

That did not surprise Lacey. Her mouth had begun watering as soon as she smelled the food. She had spent many of her summers eating bunkhouse food, and this was very similar.

Riordan, Proctor, and Willie Morse came in from outside, Proctor and Willie taking their places at the table as Riordan said, "The horses will be changed in just a few minutes, folks. Eat hearty, and you'll be on your way before you know it."

Lacey saw a look of despair pass over Eleanora's face. She knew it would be perfectly all right with Eleanora if they stayed longer at the way station. Every minute not spent in the rocking, bouncing coach would be a relief to her.

But every minute of delay also meant it would be that much longer until they reached the Rafter E. Lacey was anxious to see her father again, anxious to introduce him to Allen. She hoped that once they arrived at the ranch, Allen would begin to enjoy himself more.

But an ominous thought had already occurred to her. What if he continued to despise Texas and all it stood for? He would never want to live here, and she had resigned herself to that, but what if he refused even to come back for visits and forbade her to come alone? Could she stand never seeing her father and the ranch again?

"By the way, Ben," Riordan said, stopping beside the driver's chair, "I've got a couple more passengers for you."

Proctor looked around the room. "Where are they?"

"They were worn out, so I let 'em rest up in the barn. I'll go roust them out."

Riordan left through the rear door of the station and came back a few minutes later with a man and a boy. The man was in his late twenties, the boy around eight years old. The resemblance between them was obvious. Both had black hair, dark eyes, and olive skin. The man wore the clothes of a vaquero and carried a felt sombrero. The boy was dressed in a plain woolen suit and white shirt. He rubbed sleepily at his eyes and smiled at the people seated around the table.

"Hello," the boy said. "Are you going on the stage-coach with us?"

Lacey was the only one who smiled back at him. "Yes, we are," she said. "My name is Lacey. What's your name?" She ignored Allen's slight frown, which seemed to indicate that he disapproved of her talking to Mexicans.

The man put his hand on the boy's shoulder and ducked his head deferentially. "I am Antonio Lopez, señorita, and this is my son, Ricardo."

"Rico," the boy amended.

"Well, I'm glad to meet you, Rico," Lacey said. "And you, too, Mr. Lopez."

Ben Proctor looked up from his bowl of stew, glared at Antonio and Rico Lopez, and then swung his hard eyes over to Riordan. "What about it?" he snapped. "They got tickets?"

Riordan shrugged. "They had the money. That was good enough for me."

"Well, it ain't for me." Proctor shoved his chair back and stood up. "Greasers don't ride in my coach."

Willie Morse got to his feet and said in a low voice, "They've got tickets, Ben. We've got to let 'em ride."

Proctor regarded Antonio and Rico with narrowed eyes and then rubbed a hand over his grizzled jaw. Finally, he said, "They can ride on top. They ain't ridin' inside with the white folks."

Antonio's face had tightened into a mask at being called a greaser. He made an obvious effort to hold on to his temper as he said, "Our tickets say we can ride inside, señor."

"I drive the damned coach, and I say you can't!" Proctor snapped. "You want to argue with me, boy, you can just walk to wherever the hell you're going."

The passengers watched this exchange with varying degrees of interest. Lacey felt a flush of anger at Proctor's callous words. She could imagine how Antonio Lopez felt, being talked to that way in front of his son. Eleanora looked vaguely repulsed by the whole situation.

Antonio Lopez tried to protest once more, but Proctor turned away with a growled, "You heard me, greaser."

Allen Kerry came to his feet. He thought that Proctor was being unnecessarily rude, though he did not relish the idea of sharing the coach with Mexicans. "See here, Mr. Proctor," he said sharply, "there's no call for that kind of talk. You're being very unfair to these people."

Proctor snorted in contempt and then stalked toward the door.

Allen had started to take a step after Proctor when Louis Shepherd, who had continued eating and showed little interest in the argument, stopped him with a quiet, "You'd best let it lie, Mr. Kerry."

Allen glanced at him. "What do you mean?"

"I mean that a lot of folks out here still remember the Alamo," Shepherd told him. "Proctor must be one of them. Riding on top's better than walking."

Proctor stomped out the door, Willie Morse following him with a quick helpless glance back over his shoulder. Allen took a deep breath, sighed, and sat down, not looking at the Lopezes. He clearly did not know what else to do; he had followed a basically decent impulse and accomplished nothing.

Lacey felt a surge of pride in her fiancé, regardless of the outcome. Allen had stood up to Proctor, and that counted for something. She was glad, however, that he had not pushed it any further. Proctor struck her as the type of man who could explode into violence with very little warning. Of course, at the same time she would have liked to give Proctor a piece of her mind. He had no right to humiliate Antonio Lopez.

To change the subject, Lacey said, "Have you and your son eaten, Mr. Lopez?"

Antonio smiled and nodded. "Sí, right after we got here. Then Rico, he was sleepy . . ."

"I was not the only one who was sleepy, Papa," Rico put in, and his father chuckled.

A few minutes still remained before the stage pulled out. Antonio and Rico sat down on the same side of the table as Lacey and Allen, though Antonio was careful to leave several empty chairs between himself and Lacey. She was about to ask him where he and Rico were headed when a sudden clatter of hooves from outside caught the attention of everyone in the room. The hoofbeats were followed by profane shouts and the creak of wagon wheels.

Everyone except Eleanora got up from the table and went to the door to see what was causing the

commotion. When Lacey stepped outside and saw a
group of mounted men riding up to the station accompanied by two large wagons, each pulled by four mules,
she knew who the newcomers were—buffalo hunters.

Even back in Boston, Lacey tried to keep up with
what was occurring out west, and she knew that mil-
lions of buffalo had been slaughtered over the last few
years. Now the great herds that had filled the entire
middle section of the continent were rapidly dwindling.
As the remaining buffalo drifted south in an instinctive
effort to escape the hunters' guns, the center of the
hunting activity shifted as well. Lacey had learned that
one of the largest remaining herds had moved into the
Texas Panhandle over the last few months. Like beasts
of prey, the hunters had followed.

There were over a dozen men in this group, wear-
ing everything from shabby city clothes to buckskins.
They were heavily armed, each man carrying at least
one handgun and one rifle. Many of them had a lighter
carbine in addition to the heavy Sharps buffalo rifles,
and most had knives belted at their waists.

A few men rode on the wagons, one of which was
being driven, to Lacey's surprise, by a woman. These
were the skinners, who would strip the buffalo of their
hides once they were dead. The woman drove the lead
wagon, and as she pulled it to a halt several yards away
from the stagecoach, Lacey saw that she was young,
maybe not much older than Lacey's own twenty-one
years. But she looked tired and worn and faded, and
that made her appear older.

One of the hunters on horseback spurred ahead of
the rest and came to a stop in front of Riordan, who had
seen the group coming. He was a small man, though
the heavy coat he wore made it hard to determine his
true size. His eyes were deep set under heavy brows,
and his shaggy hair and scraggly beard gave his face a
slightly feral look. He looked arrogantly down at Riordan
and said, "Reckon you could spare some water and
grain for our horses, mister?"

"Well, I suppose I could sell you some grain,"

Riordan said. "You and your men can help yourselves
to the water. I've got a good well here."

"That's what we heard." The buffalo hunter turned
in his saddle and raised his voice. "You heard the man.
Let's get these horses taken care of." Then he swung
down, revealing that he stood a good half foot shorter
than the stationmaster. "Name's Burl Wayne," he said.
"I'm headin' up this outfit."

Behind him, his men were also dismounting and
tending to their horses and to the small remuda of extra
mounts, among which were the skinners' own saddle
horses. Lacey saw the woman climb down wearily from
the seat of the wagon.

"Look at that poor creature," Eleanora said from
beside Lacey. Her voice was pitched loudly enough
that the woman could have overheard, but if she did,
she gave no sign of it. Eleanora continued, "Imagine
what kind of squalid existence she must have."

"I'd wager it's no picnic," Lacey replied quietly.

"Typical of this godforsaken frontier," Allen put in.

Lacey sighed. She had no doubt that Allen hated
Texas.

"All right, time to get rollin'," Proctor called from
the box of the stage. "We're already far enough behind
schedule."

The four passengers started forward across the yard
toward the coach. As they did so, one of the hide
skinners leaped down from the wagon where he had
been riding, paying no attention to the mud that splashed
on his already filthy boots and pants. He looked at the
passengers, and a whistle escaped his lips. "Whooo-
eee!" he said loudly to no one in particular. "That's a
mighty pretty filly."

"Oh!" Eleanora gasped in reaction to the remark.
She increased her pace, in a hurry now to get back
aboard the stagecoach.

Lacey glanced over her shoulder and saw that,
contrary to what Eleanora obviously thought, the man's
eyes were fixed on herself. Allen's hand tightened on
her arm as he hurried her toward the coach.

Lacey was not particularly upset. She had been

around enough cowhands in her life to know that the skinner probably did not mean anything by his remark. It was just a sort of rough humor.

The skinner's next words put a different complexion on things. He spat, laughed, and said, "Reckon that little gal could sure warm up a man's blankets at night. How about it, darlin'? You want to go buffler huntin' with ol' Mick?"

Lacey blushed, partly in embarrassment and partly in anger. If Allen had not been there, she would have told off the skinner in language he would understand. But Allen would have been too shocked that she even knew such words, let alone used them.

One of the hunters who had not dismounted yet spurred forward toward the skinner. The man heard him coming and glanced over his shoulder, but he did not have time to get out of the way.

The mounted man reached down and grabbed the skinner's coat collar. The powerful muscles in his broad shoulders bunched, and with an effort that looked deceptively easy, he flung the skinner facedown into the puddle of mud chewed up by the horses' hooves. The skinner landed with a yelp and a splat.

"Shouldn't be talking to ladies that way, Mick," the hunter drawled. He was a tall man in buckskins, with a thick mane of reddish-brown hair and a mustache that drooped over his wide mouth. Though not what was commonly called handsome, he had a certain dignity about him that made him attractive.

Furious, the skinner leaped to his feet as his companions hooted and jeered at him. He was sputtering in rage as he wiped the mud from his mouth. He looked up at the tall man, who was watching him calmly, and his face paled under the coating of filth.

"You bastard!" he yelled, and his hands went for the knife at his belt. He yanked the blade out and started toward the hunter.

The buckskin-clad man lifted his right leg and dropped easily from the saddle, landing with a grace unusual in such a big man. He put his hand on the hilt of the bowie knife he carried.

"Come ahead, Mick," he said softly, the hint of a wild, reckless smile curling the corners of his mouth.

The skinner stopped in his tracks and remained still for a moment, then lifted his hands in a placating gesture. "Hold on there, now," he said. "No call for any real trouble." He noticed that he was still holding the knife and hurriedly slipped it behind his belt.

"All right, then," the hunter said with a curt nod. He turned his attention to his horse, putting his back to the skinner as if the man was not worth worrying about.

The stage passengers had stopped to watch this drama. Now that it seemed to be over, Allen again gripped Lacey's arm and muttered, "We'd better get on the coach."

This time Shepherd was waiting and ready when Eleanora stepped up into the stage. Taking her arm and assisting her, he was rewarded with another smile.

Allen helped Lacey into the coach, and then he and Shepherd climbed aboard. The Lopezes clambered on top, Antonio carrying a battered carpetbag that held all their possessions. When everyone was set, Ben Proctor popped his whip and sent the team into its jerking, jolting motion.

"My goodness, I thought those men were going to kill each other," Eleanora said as the coach settled into its usual rhythm.

"I'd say that wouldn't have been any great loss," Allen commented. "They both looked like barbarians."

"A lot of these buffalo hunters are pretty touchy," Shepherd put in. "I'm not sure they're fit to live with civilized people."

Lacey felt herself getting angry. The big man in buckskins had been defending her the best way he knew how, and she certainly did not think he had looked like a barbarian. She said, "I thought you made your living selling the Good Book, Mr. Shepherd."

Shepherd frowned at her in puzzlement. "That I do, Miss Ellis. But I'm afraid I don't see the connection between God's word and those buffalo hunters."

"Then you should take the time to read the books

instead of just selling them," Lacey replied coldly. "Somewhere in there it says *Love thy neighbor*."

Shepherd stiffened, and Lacey knew she had offended him, but at the moment she did not care. She had seen the way the man had been trying all day to get on Eleanora's good side, and she had him pegged as an opportunist.

"Really, Lacey, I can't see why you're defending the behavior of a couple of hooligans," Allen said.

"Neither can I, dear," Eleanora added tartly. "After all, they were insulting us."

"I wasn't defending both of them. And only one of them was being insulting," Lacey pointed out.

"They're all cut from the same cloth," Allen said. "It's been the same everywhere we've been. Whether it's our driver up there showing his prejudice or two roughnecks brawling in the mud, someone is always demonstrating what a crude, violent place this is."

"You're absolutely right," Eleanora sniffed.

Lacey recognized the stubbornness in their voices. She had hoped on this trip to show Allen and his sister the virtues of the state she loved, but so far all they had seen were its shortcomings—and all they were willing to see were its faults.

Lacey's visions of future visits to her father's ranch were slipping away. Maybe coming out here had not been such a good idea after all.

Chapter Two

Thirty minutes after the stagecoach rolled away from the way station, the group of buffalo hunters mounted up again. Their horses had been grained and watered and rested for a few minutes, and now they were ready to push on. The leader of the group, Burl Wayne, settled up with Riordan, though he acted as if it caused him physical pain to dole out the gold coins to the stationmaster.

As Tucker McCall swung up into the saddle and spurred his horse into motion, he felt eyes watching him. Without turning around, he knew that the gaze boring into his back belonged to the hide skinner called Mick.

Tucker supposed he should not have thrown the man in the mud, but he had gotten annoyed when Mick started harassing the women from the stage. Maybe deep down he was a gentleman.

A smile creased Tucker's face at that thought. Nobody had accused him of being a gentleman for a long time. Never, come to think of it, at least not that he could remember.

The group of hunters strung out as they left the way station behind and headed south across the plains. As the chief scout for the hunters, Tucker moved toward the front, where Burl Wayne rode. When his horse pulled up even with Wayne's, the small man glanced over at Tucker and grimaced. "I don't like my men fightin' with each other, McCall," Wayne said.

"We've got enough to worry about out here without any hard feelin's. Only reason I'm sayin' anything is because you ain't been with us long. I figure you may not know yet what I'll stand for and what I won't."

Tucker McCall frowned. In the two weeks he had known Burl Wayne, he had come to realize that he did not like the man, not one bit.

Tucker had ridden into Dodge hoping to hook up with one of the outfits heading south to the Panhandle, and at first the group led by Burl Wayne had not seemed like such a bad choice. Wayne had offered him a fair share for his services as a scout, and Tucker had accepted. He had wondered at the time just how a man of Wayne's stature managed to keep rein on his men, all of whom were bigger and stronger, but one night in a Dodge City saloon had answered that question. A burly townsman had tried to have some fun at Wayne's expense and wound up getting cut pretty badly for his trouble. Wayne handled a knife as well as anyone Tucker had ever seen, and he was utterly ruthless when he felt that he was being backed into a corner, whether the threat was real or imaginary.

Right now, Wayne might be feeling that Tucker's fracas with Mick represented a threat to his control over his men. If anybody in the group needed to be slapped down, Wayne apparently wanted to be the one to do it.

Tucker could not concern himself about what Wayne might be feeling, and he said simply, "I may be working for you, but I'm not one of your men."

Wayne glowered at him but did not say anything for a moment. Then he snarled, "Yeah, well, you'd better sleep with one eye open for a while. Mick might want to even up the score."

Tucker laughed shortly. "Let him try."

"Just you remember what I said." Wayne spurred his horse ahead, and Tucker let him go, not trying to catch up.

He was content for the time being to ride along and enjoy some peace and quiet. Behind him, some of

the other hunters were laughing and joking, and from
time to time one of them would sing a snatch of a
bawdy song, but Tucker paid them no attention. Instead he listened to the wind, letting his eyes rove over
the seemingly endless expanse in front of him.

He was not particularly happy to be here, hundreds of miles away from Kansas, the land he knew
best, and he knew that none of the other hunters liked
the situation very much, either. But if you were going
to hunt buffalo, you had to go where the shaggy beasts
were. The Panhandle was still part of the Great Plains.
The terrain was not too much different from what he
was used to.

Even though he did not like Burl Wayne—did not
like most of the men, to tell the truth—he had to admit
that buffalo hunters usually were not the most pleasant
company in the world. Hell, to those stagecoach passengers he probably looked just as wild and woolly as
any of the other hunters.

But the truth was, Tucker McCall was different.
Born in the East, his earliest memory was of his mother
reading and singing to him in front of the hearth in
their cabin. His father had been a farmer, unlettered
and worn from a life of hard work, but his mother had
somehow learned to read, and she had made sure that
knowledge was passed along to her son. Tucker had
gone to school over his father's objections that he needed
the boy to help him work the land, and his education
had lasted long enough to whet his appetite for learning.

Then a hard winter and a lingering fever had taken
his mother away from him, and that was the end of his
schooling.

Tucker stayed home until he was sixteen, tolerat-
ing his father and working on the farm, listening to the
elder McCall talk about how useless an education was.
All a man really needed, according to Tucker's father,
was a strong back and the realization that dreams were
an empty waste of time better spent plowing.

Tucker listened, but he did not stop dreaming.
And he read every book he could lay his hands on,

which did not amount to many. When he was sixteen, he had walked away from the farm, heading west and not looking back.

God, but that was a long time ago! He was thirty-five years old now, and more than half his life had been spent on the frontier. He had soldiered for a while, mustering out in time to miss the Civil War officially, though he had been a civilian scout for the Union army during the western campaigns and had seen his share of the fighting. Since the end of the war he had scouted at times for the army in their campaigns against the Indians, but mostly he had hunted buffalo, joining the large group of men who made a living off the massive beasts. He was a very good shot with the Sharps Big Fifty rifle that was lashed to his saddle, and his keen eyes and good sense of direction made him an excellent scout.

So far he had made a fair enough living. He did not have very many wants or responsibilities. As long as he made enough for food and gear and ammunition, plus a drink every now and then and female companionship when he felt the need, that was plenty.

Tucker knew it was not going to last, though. There was an end to everything, and he had seen it coming for a couple of years now. When you topped a rise and saw a herd of buffalo literally filling a valley, stretching to the horizon as far as the eye could see, you thought there was an endless supply of the creatures. But the buffalo were dwindling now, a dying breed—and when they were gone, what would become of men like him?

It looked as though he was a dying breed, too, he thought with a wry smile.

Burl Wayne called a halt in the middle of the afternoon as the sky was clouding up again, promising a return of the morning's cold rain. The horses were watered after being allowed to rest for a few minutes.

Wayne caught Tucker's eye and gestured for the scout to join him. "I think we'll camp here for a while," Wayne said. He nodded toward a small creek that trickled along the bottom of a slight dip in the land. "We've got water here and enough grass for a day or two . . . if you get lucky, that is. I want you to find that damn herd, McCall."

Tucker nodded, not taking offense at Wayne's harsh tone. "Do my best," he said.

"We need hides," Wayne went on. He spat and jerked a thumb at the small stack of hides on one of the wagons. "Findin' a few strays every now and then ain't gonna make money for any of us. Understand?"

"Sure. I'll fill my canteen and get some jerky from Helen's wagon and head on out. May not be back until morning."

"I don't care when you get back," Wayne snapped. "Just bring back word of them damned buffalo."

Tucker turned away from the bearded man and walked over to the wagon driven by the woman. Helen Wayne looked up at his approach, and a spark of life suddenly shone in her faded blue eyes.

"Hello, Tucker," she said. "Heading out?"

"Got to find those buffalo that keep hiding from me," Tucker said, returning her smile. "Reckon you could get some jerky and hardtack together?"

"Sure." Helen nodded. "I'd be glad to, Tucker."

"I'll be back in a few minutes then." Tucker turned away from the wagon and went to his horse to get his canteen, filling it then from the water barrel on the other wagon.

When he returned a few minutes later, leading his horse, Helen had the rough provisions ready for him. He took the small sack from her and said, "Thanks. I'll be seeing you."

"All right, Tucker. You're welcome." Her voice was much softer now than it was when she was popping the bullwhip and cursing at the mules that pulled her wagon. When it came to cussing, Tucker thought, Helen could hold her own with any driver he had run across. "You going to be back tonight?" she asked.

"I don't know," Tucker said. "Maybe. Depends on how quick I find that herd."

"Why don't you stop by and say hello when you come back in? I don't care how late it is." Helen ducked her head slightly and did not meet his eyes. "I'll be bedded down under the wagon, just like always."

Tucker was not quite sure what to say to that. He knew what she was asking, knew that she had more in mind than just saying hello. After a moment, he answered gruffly, "Reckon you need your sleep. Driving that wagon's no easy chore. Anyway, I might not be back until tomorrow morning."

Helen caught at her bottom lip with her teeth and then nodded. "Sure," she said. "I understand."

Feeling awkward, Tucker swung up into the saddle and prodded the horse into a trot that took him away from the camp to the south. Once he put a little distance behind him, he would start a long gentle curve that would take him first east, then west.

As he rode, he thought about Helen Wayne. She and Burl Wayne referred to themselves as brother and sister, but Tucker had heard the men talking enough to know that was not true. The way he had heard the story, Burl Wayne's parents had taken Helen in when she was a young child and raised her as one of their own. Her own parents had died in some sort of accident. Helen might have been a distant cousin, but the blood relationship was not any closer than that.

Tucker was certain of one thing: Not even a buffalo hunter would pimp for his own blood sister.

He had found out soon after leaving Dodge that Helen was selling her favors. A couple of the hunters visited her bedroll under the wagon every night, and it was pretty damned obvious what was going on. Out on the plains like this, Helen was the only woman these men were likely to see for weeks at a time, except maybe an Indian squaw every now and then. And compared to some of the soiled doves in the settlements, she was attractive, all right. Her body was slim and well formed, though toughened by work, and somehow she managed to keep her long, straight blond hair reasonably clean.

Still, the men would have left her alone, her being Burl Wayne's adopted sister, if Wayne himself had not encouraged her whoring.

One of the hunters had told Tucker about the arrangement one night, complaining bitterly about the price that was being exacted. No money changed hands now, but at the end of the hunt, each man who visited Helen's blankets would lose a percentage of his share to Wayne. For the time being, Wayne turned a blind eye to the proceedings, preferring to wait until the hides were sold to settle up.

If Wayne had been a different sort, Tucker might have thought that the man just did not want to admit to himself what was going on. That was not the case with Burl Wayne, though; he was always out to make a profit. Besides, he had more important things than his sister's honor on his mind.

Tucker felt sorry for Helen, yet he figured she knew what she was doing. He was sure the prostitution was her brother's idea; nevertheless, she could have said no if she had really wanted to. It would have been hard, since she had been under Wayne's thumb most of her life, but she could have done it.

In the meantime, she seemed to have a crush on Tucker McCall—and Tucker sure as hell did not know what to do about that.

Helen had made it plain on more than one occasion that she liked him, but today was the first time she had asked him to visit her under the wagon. She probably was wondering why he had not paid her a call there so far on the journey.

To tell the truth, Tucker was not sure why he had not. He did not feel any moral outrage at what she was doing—he had spent a few nights in the Dodge City brothels himself. But so far he had been friends with Helen, and he wanted to keep things on that basis. She had been disappointed when he turned her down, he could tell that, even though she had taken it gracefully enough.

Suddenly the picture in his mind changed from Helen to another young woman, with shining brunette hair and fresh, open features and eyes that had seemed to look right into him, though she had barely glanced at him back there at the stagecoach station.

Tucker did not know her name, but he could see her face as plain as day. He wondered if his thoughts of her had had anything to do with his refusal to stop at Helen Wayne's bedroll. But, he told himself, there was no use speculating on things like that. After all, he probably would never see the woman from the stagecoach again.

Lacey Ellis pulled the coarse woolen blanket around her a bit tighter. The sunshine earlier in the afternoon had not lasted long. The clouds had thickened again, cutting off what little warmth came from the sun. Lacey and Eleanora had wrapped themselves in the blankets provided by the stage line, though Eleanora looked none too pleased with the prospect. As she pointed out, there was no way of knowing who had last used the blankets.

Lacey was grateful for the warmth, but she kept thinking about Antonio Lopez and his young son riding on top of the coach. Antonio and Rico both had coats, but the garments were not heavy enough for riding in the open in weather like this. The Lopezes had to be cold.

She looked out the window beside her, peering around the canvas curtain, and saw that the rain had begun once more, coming down now in a soaking drizzle. She could not keep quiet any longer.

Leaning over to the window, she called, "Mr. Proctor!"

It was Willie Morse who hung over the side of the box and looked back at her. "What is it, Miss Ellis?" he asked, raising his voice over the coach's clatter.

Allen Kerry leaned forward with obvious concern. "What's wrong, Lacey?" he asked.

Lacey ignored her fiancé for the moment. With the mist hitting her face, she said to Willie, "Please ask Mr. Proctor to stop!"

Willie's face disappeared as he straightened up on the box. Lacey heard him speak to Proctor and then heard Proctor's profane reaction. But then the coach began to slow, and a moment later it came to a halt.

Ben Proctor climbed down from the box and jerked open the coach door. "What is it?" he snapped at Lacey.

He was trying to cow her with his gruff manner, Lacey knew, but she was angry, and she was not going to let anybody run roughshod over her. Looking him straight in the eye, she said, "You've got no right to make Señor Lopez and his boy ride on top of the coach when there's plenty of room in here. Especially not in weather like this!"

Proctor returned her glower with one of his own and began to say, "It's my coach and—"

"No, it's not!" Lacey interrupted him. "It belongs to the express company, and you can be sure I'll be talking to their district manager when we reach San Angelo."

"Lacey . . ." Allen said, then shook his head without saying anything more. He had seen that look on Lacey's face before and knew she was not going to be thwarted.

"Really, Lacey, don't make a scene!" Eleanora scolded. "After all, Mr. Proctor is our driver. I'm sure he knows what he's doing."

And you don't want to share the coach with a couple of Mexicans, Lacey thought as she glanced at Eleanora. She returned her attention to Proctor and said, "Well? Are you going to let those people get in out of the rain or not?"

Proctor regarded her with narrowed eyes. "What if I don't?"

"Then I'll climb up there and ride with them."

"Lacey! You wouldn't!" Eleanor said, obviously scandalized at the prospect.

Allen spoke up again. "Really, Lacey, there's no need for that. I'm sure we can come to some sort of agreement."

Proctor rubbed at his jaw, his gloved palm rasping on the beard stubble there. "Your daddy's Sam Ellis, ain't he?"

"He is," Lacey confirmed. "Do you know him?"

"Heard of him." Abruptly, Proctor looked up at the top of the coach, where Antonio and Rico were

huddled together. "All right, you two, get on down
here and climb inside. I want to get this damned
coach rollin' again. Nothin' but a bunch of goddamn
delays . . ."

Proctor continued to mutter as he hauled himself
back up on the box.

As Antonio and Rico were climbing down, Willie
Morse hopped off the box long enough to open the rear
boot so that Antonio could stow his carpetbag there.
When Antonio and Rico had boarded the coach, Proctor
popped the whip and got the team under way again.

As the stage lurched into motion, Antonio and Rico
sat gratefully on the center bench. Their clothing was
already wet, and Rico was shivering slightly as his father put his arm around his shoulders.

"Here," Lacey said, offering them the blanket she
had been using. "Maybe you can warm up a bit with
this."

Antonio took the blanket and wrapped it around
Rico. "Gracias, señorita. I will be all right, but the boy,
he is cold."

Lacey looked over at Eleanora, hoping she might
surrender her own blanket, but the older woman made
no move to do so. She might not have known who used
it last, but she was not prepared to give it up now.

There was a touch of admiration in Allen's eyes as
he looked at Lacey. Though her method had been a bit
extreme, she had accomplished what he had failed to
back at the way station: getting fair treatment for the
young father and son.

Lacey noticed that Eleanora regarded the Lopezes
disdainfully for a moment and then looked away, as though
it was her intention to ignore them as much as possible.

Within a few minutes, Rico's shivering stopped.
Both he and his father seemed to be warming up, and
there was affection in the boy's gaze as he looked at
Lacey. He probably missed his mother, she thought,
and the friendliness of a woman was very welcome right
now.

"Feeling better?" Lacey asked the older Lopez
with a smile.

"*Sí*, much better," Antonio answered. "It was getting very cold up there."

"I'm glad you were able to come in. I don't believe you mentioned where you and Rico are going."

Antonio smiled, and Lacey knew he was glad for the opportunity to make conversation. "We are bound for San Antonio. The blessed saint and I, we share the same name, eh, but little else."

Lacey said nothing but continued to smile, encouraging Antonio to go on.

"I have family there, an uncle and aunt and many cousins. My uncle, he owns a *restaurante*. I will work for him there."

"I thought from your clothes that you were a vaquero."

Antonio nodded. "*Sí*, I was. We lived on a small cattle ranch west of the way station where we boarded the stage. My uncle had written asking me to work for him, and when—"

Antonio broke off suddenly and looked down at Rico. The boy was leaning against him, his head resting on his father's shoulder, and his eyes were closed. Antonio smiled at his sleeping son.

"And when my wife was taken from us," he went on in a soft voice, "I decided it would be better for Rico to grow up in a place where there were other children, where there is laughter and much love. A ranch is no place for a boy with no mother."

"I'm sorry about your wife," Lacey said sincerely. "What happened?"

"A fever of some sort. There was no time to bring a doctor, even if one had been close. But there are no doctors in our region. It was the will of God, and Rico and I have accepted it."

But it still hurt, that much was obvious. As Antonio's story had unfolded, Lacey felt her heart going out to him, and even Eleanora had unbent enough to look sympathetic.

Allen said, "It sounds like you made the right decision to move, Mr. Lopez. I hope you and Rico are happy in San Antonio."

Antonio's smile brightened. "I am sure we will be."

Lacey was glad Allen had spoken politely. Antonio and Rico needed friends right now.

Up on the box, Willie Morse was dozing when Ben Proctor's elbow suddenly dug sharply into his ribs. Willie jerked awake, his hands tightening on the grip of his shotgun.

"What is it?" he asked Proctor.

Proctor nodded to the right. "Look off over there," he directed.

Willie did so, and he felt his heart begin to pound harder against his ribs.

The mist cut down on visibility, but a slight rise about a hundred yards to the west was still visible. Five riders sat there on horseback. Though the distance was too great to make out any details, Proctor and Willie were both sure that the riders were Indians.

Willie swallowed nervously. "What do you think, Ben?"

"Comanches, more'n likely." He grimaced, and his slitted eyes studied the five figures. "Don't look like they're movin', though."

"You think they'll come after us?"

Proctor did not answer right away. He kept the team moving at a steady pace. Whipping them up right now might just draw the Indians on. No use waving a red flag at them.

The stage drew even with the Indians and then passed them, and still the horses remained on the rise. Willie turned his head to watch. Despite his youth, he was no green kid; he had fought Indians and bandits before and knew how to handle the rifle under his slicker. But only a fool would not be scared out here on the prairie with the Comanches on the prowl.

"They're not following," Willie suddenly said. As he watched, the Indians turned their horses and vanished over the other side of the rise. "They're leaving!" Willie exclaimed, his voice rising with excitement.

Proctor snaked out the whip and popped it, sending the team into a harder gallop. "We'd best make the time while we can," he grated. "They must've thought this weather was bad medicine, but we ain't gonna be that lucky twice. It's another four miles to the next way station. I'm gonna make damn sure we get there before nightfall."

Chapter Three

Tucker McCall did not mind being alone on the plains. Solitude did not bother him; he was satisfied with his own company most of the time. Likewise, he was confident in his ability to take care of himself.

But a man sure had a lot of time to think when he was off by himself like this.

It was late afternoon now, and he had put several miles between himself and the buffalo hunters' camp. So far, he had not come across any buffalo sign except a couple of old mud wallows that appeared not to have been used for weeks.

As the weather grew colder, he unrolled the coat that was tied behind his saddle and slipped it on. The slow, steady rain started again not long after.

Tucker found as he rode along that he could not get that young woman's face out of his mind. He wondered what her name was, where she was coming from, and where she was going. And he wondered if one of the two male passengers was her husband. Not that it mattered; he was just curious.

Unbidden, his thoughts went back to the time he had come west, and as he recalled those long years, he realized that they had been pretty well devoid of any feeling other than the drive for survival. Oh, he had derived some satisfaction from knowing that he was good at his work, and at times he had felt a certain savage pleasure in a saloon brawl. But he had had no close friends, and his relationships with women had been strictly physical, flings quickly forgotten and meaning little. It was as if genuine emotion had died along with his mother.

Tucker rode into a broad, shallow valley. In the center of it, judging from the brush, was a small creek that had water in it this time of year. No doubt in summer it would be dry, but right now it was a live stream.

His breath caught in his throat as he saw the animals covering the plains on either side of the creek, and he felt a surge of excitement. He had found the herd!

Compared to some of the massive herds he had seen in Kansas, this was a small one. His experienced eyes scanned the scene and set the number somewhere between thirty-five hundred and five thousand. But the herd would furnish a good kill, especially for this time and this place.

As he sat his horse and looked down across the valley at the grazing animals, he almost felt sorry for them. They had been driven down here by the gun, and now they were running out of room. The herds would continue to drift south, but Tucker doubted that many of them would ever reach Mexico, not that they would be safe even if they did.

When the buffalo were gone, that would be the end of them, the end of a lot of things.

Regardless of that, Tucker McCall had a job to do. He scanned from horizon to horizon, noting what few landmarks there were. He was not too worried about finding his way back here; he could do that easily enough, after years of scouting. After another long look, he turned his horse's head back toward the north and spurred it into a fast trot.

Dusk closed in around him, the overcast sky making night fall sooner than it normally would have. As Tucker rode, he began to feel a crawling sensation in his back. It was a feeling he had experienced before.

He was being watched.

Turning in the saddle, he searched the gathering

shadows of his back trail. There was nothing to be seen, but the feeling persisted. He stepped up the pace. He was not going to ignore the warning his instincts were sending him.

Then a sharp, fluttering whisper raced by his head, inches from his ears. Instantly, Tucker bent forward over the neck of his horse and spurred the animal into a gallop. He knew that an arrow had just narrowly missed him.

Bloodthirsty whoops sounded behind him, and he turned his head to see three Indians on ponies burst out of a draw thirty yards behind him. More arrows flew by him, fired with remarkable accuracy considering the conditions.

There was no time to be scared, no time for anything except flight. Tucker knew that with his Winchester he could turn and face them and probably down at least two of them, maybe all three. But there was no way of knowing how many other braves were nearby. And shots would draw the attention of any other Indians in the area.

He had a good horse. Maybe, just maybe, he could outrun them.

At that moment his horse fell out from under him, and Tucker suddenly was flying through the air, going head over heels. He had a crazy vision of the world turning upside down. A part of his brain that was still rational knew that the horse had stepped into a hole and stumbled.

Then he plowed into the ground, landing heavily and rolling several times before he came to a stop, the breath knocked out of him. He gasped for air and tasted dirt in his mouth.

The exultant cries of his attackers drove awareness back into his brain. He looked up and saw his horse floundering awkwardly on the ground several feet away, though he could not tell how badly the animal was hurt. His eyes flicked to the Indians and saw that they were nearly upon him.

The saddle boot holding his Winchester was on top

of the horse's side, and Tucker realized that with the
rifle he still had a chance. If it had been trapped underneath the horse, he would not have been able to put up
a fight.

Ignoring the pounding in his head and the pain in
his shoulder and side, he came up on hands and knees
and lunged toward the horse in a long dive, avoiding
the flailing hooves. He reached out, feeling the smooth
wooden stock of the rifle under his fingers.

Jerking the weapon free of the boot, he rolled over
as an arrow thudded into the sod next to him, its shaft
quivering with the impact. He levered a shell into the
chamber and pulled the trigger, firing without aiming
as the Indians flashed by him.

Tucker's first shot missed, but as the Comanches
tried to rein in their horses and turn around, he came
up on his knees and fired again. The light was bad and
his head was spinning, but the shot went home. One of
the Indians cried out and slumped in the saddle.

Tucker worked the lever and fired, then fired again.
If they wanted his scalp, then by God they would have
to work for it!

The Indians must have decided it was not worth it,
for at that moment they wheeled their horses and broke
into a gallop. The pony carrying the wounded brave
followed along in the wake of the others. Tucker sent a
couple more shots after them in the gloom and then got
a grip on himself. The Indians were gone; no use wast-
ing lead firing at phantoms in the mist.

He got to his feet and looked around. To his surprise, his horse was also on its feet. It must have just
stumbled instead of stepping into a hole, as Tucker had
thought. Accustomed to barrages of gunfire from the
hunts it had been on, it had not bolted during the
battle. Speaking to it in a soft voice, Tucker examined
the animal and found no serious injuries. That was a
miracle, he thought; he had expected a broken leg.

Now he was going to try to compound that miracle
and get out of there before the shooting drew any other
Indians. He scooped his hat from the ground and stepped

up into the saddle, sliding the Winchester back into the boot. It took him a moment to reorient himself, and then he headed north at a gallop.

He saw the light from a campfire long before he reached it. The rain had stopped again, and the clouds were breaking up, stars occasionally showing through the gaps. Somewhere the hunters had scrounged up enough dry wood for a fire, and it was blazing nicely, lighting up the night. Indians did not attack at night except under unusual circumstances, especially not against a large, well-armed force like this one.

Burl Wayne was waiting at the edge of the circle of light, a rifle cocked and ready in his hands. When Tucker rode in, his horse's pace a weary walk, Wayne fell into step beside him.

"Find 'em?" Wayne asked brusquely.

Tucker nodded. "I found them. They're about six miles south of here, along a little creek." The fact that Wayne had not asked him if he had had any trouble was no surprise.

"How many?"

"At least thirty-five hundred, maybe as many as five thousand."

Wayne clenched his free hand into a fist. "I knew I'd find them! I want those hides, McCall. This may be the last hunt. I've got to make it now or not at all."

With Wayne at his side, Tucker rode to the rope corral and dismounted. Then he turned his horse in with the others after stripping the saddle from it. All he wanted now was some hot food and a cup of coffee, not to listen to Burl Wayne's greed. But he did owe it to the head of the outfit to inform him about the Comanches he had run into.

"We'll keep our base camp here," Wayne said after Tucker told him about the Indians. "And we'll start the hunt early in the mornin'. You be ready to take us there."

"I will be," Tucker told him.

He walked toward the fire, leaving Wayne to antic-ipate the next day's slaughter. Most of the hunters were

still awake, lingering over a final cup of coffee and a
cigarette. Tucker did not see Helen Wayne by the fire,
and as he passed beside her wagon, he heard her voice.

"See, it's not too late, Tucker."

She came from under the wagon, a blanket around
her shoulders. The fire lit her face with a flickering
glow. Tucker saw how intently she was looking at him,
and he realized that he had been hoping she would be
asleep when he returned to camp.

"Hello, Helen," he said, smiling tiredly at her.

Suddenly she noticed a scrape on his face and a
ragged hole torn in his buckskin shirt. She stepped
forward, lifting a hand. "You've been hurt!" she exclaimed.

Tucker shook his head. "It's nothing to worry about."

"What happened?"

He hesitated a moment and then decided to tell
her the truth. As a member of the company, she deserved to know what was going on. "I had a run-in with
some Comanches," he said.

Helen might have paled a bit; it was hard to tell in
the uncertain light. "You're all right, though?"

"I'm fine."

"What happened to the Indians?"

"I winged one, and all three took off."

She rested her hand on his arm. "Can I get you
anything?"

"I just want some food and coffee."

"You go sit by the fire. I'll bring you some."

There did not seem to be any way of refusing that,
so Tucker did as she said. Several of the hunters greeted
him as he sat down cross-legged near the fire. The
warmth felt good.

"Find the herd?" one of the hunters asked.

Tucker nodded. "South of here. We'll move out
early in the morning, Wayne says."

The man made noises of relief and agreement.
They had begun to worry that this trip down here from
Kansas had been for nothing.

Helen came to the fire carrying a plate of beans
and a mug of coffee, both of which had been warmed

over the smaller cooking fire several yards away. Tucker
reached up, took the food, and said, "Thanks."

Helen sank down on her knees beside him. Tucker
waited a second to see if she was going to say or do
anything, and when she did not, he began to eat. There
was something uncomfortably domestic about the way
she sat quietly there beside him.

She spoke up a few minutes later when Burl Wayne
walked up to the campfire. Looking up at her adopted
brother, she said, "Burl, did Tucker tell you about the
Indians?"

Wayne glanced at Tucker, anger flaring in his eyes.
He would have preferred that his men did not know
anything about any Indian trouble. "He told me," Wayne
said curtly. "I don't think it's anythin' to worry about."

"What's this about Injuns?" one of the other hunters asked as he came to his feet.

Wayne swung around to glare at the man. "Nothin'
to worry about, I told you! McCall just ran into some
redskins."

"Comanches, I'd say," Tucker put in quietly.
"Looked to me like they were painted for war."

The word spread quickly then, racing through the
camp in muttered comments. When Tucker saw Wayne
looking at him, he returned the man's cold stare. All he
had done was tell the truth, and he was not going to
worry about what Wayne thought.

Wayne raised his voice, cutting through the speculation. "We move out two hours before dawn," he said.
"You all better get some sleep, 'cause your shots have
to count tomorrow. Don't forget that." He turned and
stalked away from the fire, heading for his own bedroll.

Tucker watched him go and then heard Helen say,
"We're heading right into trouble, aren't we, Tucker?"

"I don't know. I never heard tell of Indians attacking a group of hunters this big. It's always the small
bunches, two or three men, who wind up massacred. If
enough Indians got together, though, there's no telling
what they might do."

"No telling," Helen repeated in a voice little more
than a whisper.

*   *   *

The way station was a welcome sight to the people aboard the stagecoach. The coach pulled into the yard in the thickening dusk, and the glow of light from the station's windows was warm and welcoming.

The stationmaster, a tall bearded man who had no apparent first name and went by the single name Mertz, was waiting for them. He came up to the stage and opened the door for the passengers. Then he said to Proctor, "You're running a mite late, Ben. Weather slow you up?"

Proctor's reply was laced with profane references to Texas weather. He climbed down from the box, saw the hostlers hurrying from the barn to begin the task of changing the teams, and said sharply, "Leave 'em be. I ain't goin' any further tonight."

"But, Ben, the schedule—" Willie Morse began.

"Hang the schedule! We're already late, ain't we? I'm not drivin' in the dark, not with the roads the way they are. If we was to stray off, the coach would bog right down in the mud."

"Reckon that would be sort of risky, what with the Indian trouble," Mertz said. "Rain's letting up a lot. Maybe if it'll stop and hold off until morning, things'll dry out." Mertz instructed the hostlers to move the coach into the barn and then to go ahead and unhitch the team, saying they could take their time now.

The passengers had disembarked by now and were walking toward the station. It was much like the last one, a low, flat-roofed adobe building with a corral and barn out back. The six passengers went inside and found food and coffee waiting. Mertz was not married, and he prepared the meals himself; the fare was simpler and less appetizing, but none of the passengers turned their noses up at it, not even Eleanora.

When Proctor and Willie came inside a few minutes later, followed by Mertz, Allen asked the driver, "How long will we be stopped here, Mr. Proctor?"

"Till mornin'," Proctor answered.

"We weren't scheduled to stop here overnight," Lacey said in surprise.

"Schedule or no schedule, I ain't drivin' in the dark, not with the roads bein' bad."

Eleanora looked around at her surroundings. The furniture was primitive and rough-hewn, and buffalo rugs were scattered on the floor, which was simply pounded dirt. There were no windows, only slits for the rifles in case of attack. Eleanora considered the situation and then said, "We have to spend the night *here*?"

"It's not so bad," Lacey told her. "At least there's a roof over our heads. I remember sleeping out in a bedroll under the stars once when visiting my father." Lacey paused thoughtfully. "Actually, that wasn't so bad."

"I'm sure it wasn't, dear, for you. I'm afraid I simply couldn't survive under such conditions."

That was probably true, Lacey mused. The frontier would chew Eleanora up and spit her out.

"This doesn't seem much worse than the last way station where we stayed," Allen put in. "A bit crude, perhaps, but not too bad."

Mertz bristled, his pride as stationmaster wounded by these uppity eastern folks. "See here, mister," he began, "this is the best station on the line—"

"Let it lay, Mertz," Proctor said in a bored voice as he dug into the dried meat and beans that Mertz had prepared. "Sometimes talkin' don't do any good."

Allen looked angrily at the grizzled driver. "I'm not sure what you mean by that, sir."

Proctor said, "I mean we're here and there ain't no use talkin' about it. We're not goin' on until it's safer. I sure as hell don't want to be stuck out there at night."

Lacey thought there was more to his words than what he let on. Quickly, she asked, "What do you mean, Mr. Proctor? Is there some trouble you haven't told us about?"

Proctor shook his head. "No trouble. I just want to keep it that way."

Lacey could tell he was lying. The others might not realize it, but she did.

The tired, hungry passengers ate heartily, and then

Mertz and Willie Morse went outside to check on the horses. Proctor pulled a foul-smelling pipe from his pocket and settled down in front of the stove to pack and light it.

After a few moments, Eleanora stood up and said, "Lacey, may I speak to you in private?"

"Of course." Lacey got up and followed Eleanora to the corner farthest from the others.

In a whisper, Eleanora asked the question that had been bothering her ever since she found out they were staying the night here. "Lacey, where are we all going to sleep?" She was flushed with embarrassment as she posed the question.

Lacey tried not to let Eleanora see the smile tugging at her mouth. She looked around the one room of the station, which took up the whole building. There was a cot in one corner where Mertz slept; the hostlers probably bedded down in the barn.

"I don't know about you," Lacey said, "but I intend to wrap up in a blanket and sleep on one of those benches at the table. It's not much, but it beats the cold floor."

Eleanora looked as though she might break down and start crying at any moment. "Why did I ever come out here?" she asked in a low moan. "Why did you talk my brother into coming? Couldn't you have just left us alone where we were comfortable?"

Lacey felt a surge of anger. "Allen and I are going to be married," she said quietly. "I want him to meet my father. And you're the one who insisted that we needed a chaperone, Eleanora."

"Well, I was right, wasn't I?" Eleanora shot back. "You may know all about . . . *cows* . . . but you know very little about civilized behavior."

Lacey gasped. The urge to slap Eleanora was nearly overwhelming, but she did not give in to it. That would only have given the older woman more ammunition. In a tight voice, she said, "You can think and do whatever you want, Eleanora. *I'm* going to try to get as much sleep as I can."

Lacey turned and walked back to the table.

Allen watched her with obvious concern, having overheard enough to know that Lacey and Eleanora had been arguing. As Lacey sat down beside him, he asked, "Are you all right?"

"I'm fine, Allen," Lacey replied. "I'm not so sure about your sister."

Eleanora was still standing in the corner, chewing on one of her knuckles and staring at the floor. She wanted to scream and rage at the cruel fate that had brought her here to this wilderness, but she was sensible enough to know that it would not do any good. She was thousands of miles away from home, alone except for Allen, and he was too much in love even to consider how his only sister felt.

She became aware that someone was standing beside her and looked up to see Louis Shepherd. He was watching her with those warm, sensitive eyes, and as her gaze met his, he said, "I know this is all very difficult for you, Mrs. Morrison. You're not accustomed to a life like this, and a lady such as yourself shouldn't be subjected to these hardships. If there's anything I can do to help . . ."

She had been wrong, Eleanora thought. She was not alone except for Allen. Louis Shepherd was a gentleman, and he understood how a lady felt about things.

She caught at her lip and said, "Thank you, Mr. Shepherd. I . . . I'm sure I'll be all right."

"I'm sure you will be, too. But just remember that you can call on me at any time . . . Eleanora."

She smiled, surprised but at the same time pleased by his forwardness. She said, "I'll remember that . . . Louis."

Louis, Eleanora thought. *Sweet Louis . . .*

At the table, Allen turned to Lacey. "I wish you and Eleanora got along better, Lacey. After all, you are going to be sisters."

"I know, Allen." Lacey sighed. "I'll try."

"What were the two of you talking about?"

"She was worried about the sleeping arrangements."

Lacey saw Allen frown as she answered him, and she knew that he thought she was too plainspoken. It was not genteel to discuss such things—but dammit, he did ask her what the argument was about!

"This trip has had more than its share of problems, all right," Allen said.

Lacey looked around. They were alone at the table; Eleanora and Shepherd were still talking quietly in the corner, and Antonio and Rico were standing by the stove, ignoring the occasional hostile glance sent their way by Ben Proctor. Lacey gathered up her courage and decided to take advantage of the opportunity to speak to Allen while they had some semblance of privacy.

"Are you starting to wish you hadn't come out here, Allen?" she asked. "You don't like Texas at all, do you?"

"I haven't seen much of it yet," Allen replied with more diplomacy than was his usual custom. "Still, I don't see what appeal it has for you. I'll certainly be glad when we get back to Boston. I want to put all this behind us, so that we can get on with our lives."

Lacey's heart sank at his words. She was sure his idea of getting on with their lives did not include any more visits to Texas. "I'm sorry to hear you say that," she said quietly.

Allen regarded her intently. "You're upset. Well, I'm sorry, but I told you the way I feel." He paused for a moment, then went on, "There's something I've been wanting to talk to you about, darling."

Lacey looked up, aware that his endearment had sounded slightly hollow. She waited for him to continue.

"I've been thinking," he finally said. "I've been thinking about that man back at the other way station and the way you looked at him."

"I'm not sure I know what you mean," Lacey said, but her sudden embarrassment gave lie to that. She knew very well what he was talking about. "If you're referring to that insulting hide skinner—" she began.

"I'm not, and you know it," Allen said. "I mean the other one, the big one in buckskins who threw the skinner in the mud. I imagine you'd rather I was more like him. More a man of action."

"That's not true, Allen. I love you. I fell in love with you just the way you are."

Even as she fervently spoke the words, Lacey wondered if she was telling the truth. The buckskin-clad man had been impressive, and Allen was definitely out of place here in the West. But what did she really know about the other man? Nothing except that he had been ready to fight the skinner over a few rude comments. How could a man like that compare with a man as accomplished as Allen Kerry?

The answer was simple: He could not.

"I love you, Allen," Lacey said again when he did not reply. She told herself that she meant it, absolutely and completely. After all, Allen had tried to stand up to Proctor when the driver insisted that Antonio and Rico ride on the coach's roof. That was certainly an admirable act.

As Antonio and Rico moved away from the stove, Willie Morse and Mertz came back into the building and joined Ben Proctor by the fire. Proctor glanced at them and grunted, "Everything all right?"

"For now," Mertz said. "Willie told me about them Indians you spotted. This is shaping up to be a bad business, Ben. There's just too many of them damned red devils circulating around these days."

"What do you think we should do, Mr. Mertz?" Willie asked.

Proctor did not wait for the stationmaster to answer the question. "I'll tell you what we're goin' to do," he said. "We're goin' on south, just like we're supposed to."

"You could hole up here until this trouble blows over," Mertz suggested.

"When'll that be?" Proctor shook his head. "No way of knowin'. I ain't never been one to turn tail and run, neither. In this case, goin' back north might amount to runnin' right into those Comanches."

"Reckon you're right," Mertz agreed glumly. "Now that I think about it, staying out here don't seem like such a good idea. Suppose I'll have to, though; I've got an obligation to the company."

The three men fell silent as they mused over the situation. Proctor and Willie understood Mertz's comment about having an obligation. Out here a man stuck by what he said he would do—most of the time, anyway.

Over by the rear door of the building, Rico Lopez tugged on his father's short jacket and then whispered in Antonio's ear when he bent over. Antonio nodded and opened the door, pointing to the outhouse about a hundred feet behind the station. Rico promised to go straight there and straight back and not to wander over to the corral and the barn. Antonio stood watching with a smile on his face as his son hurried off. Then he turned back to the stove to see about getting another cup of coffee.

At the outhouse, Rico quickly tended to his business. When he left, he was not in such a hurry to get back to the station, despite the biting chill of the night air. He did not intend to disobey his father; he just wanted to look at the horses in the corral. Rico had always liked horses. This was the fresh team that would be pulling their stagecoach next.

He was still fifteen or twenty feet away when he saw the movement in the shadows next to the barn door. Someone was there, coming out of the barn, stopping suddenly at the sight of the little boy.

The clouds had broken up enough to let some starlight through. Rico's keen eyes saw the buckskins, the long braided hair, the knife in the Comanche's hand. For a moment he was too surprised to move or even to make a sound. Then the Indian lunged at him, breaking the spell.

Rico yelled and darted to the side as the Indian grabbed at him. He felt fingers grasping his coat for a moment, and then he pulled away and ran toward the house, shouting, "Papa! Papa!"

Inside the station, Antonio Lopez heard the frightened cries of his son and dropped the cup he had been holding. He ran to the back door, fear etching lines in his own face. Willie Morse, clutching his shotgun, and Ben Proctor were right on his heels.

Antonio saw Rico running toward him and hurried to meet the boy. From the doorway, Ben Proctor yelled, "Get down, greaser!" Antonio grabbed Rico, wrapping his arms around the boy and diving to the ground with him.

Shots blasted from the barn and were answered from the station. Antonio rolled out of the line of fire, taking Rico with him, and then leaped to his feet and ran to take cover behind a barrel that was sitting against the station wall.

Mertz ducked inside the station and came back with a Henry repeater in his hands. He called out to his hostlers in the barn, but there was no reply except for more shots. Then arrows began flying from the open door of the barn to thud into the thick adobe walls of the station.

Mertz fired the Henry, pouring lead into the barn. Combined with the fire from Proctor and Willie, things had to be getting hot for the intruders.

A rumble of hooves sounded from the barn, almost lost in the din of the battle.

"Watch it!" Mertz yelled. "They're going to try to bust out with the horses!"

A few seconds later, a mass of surging, frightened horseflesh suddenly appeared in the door of the barn, pausing for an instant and then bursting out into the night. Whoops filled the air as the raiding Indians rode several of the stolen horses out of the barn. Clinging to the racing horses with a precarious foothold and the fingers of one hand tangled in the manes, they fired rifles and pistols with their free hands, forcing the white men back into the station with a hail of bullets. Then abruptly they were gone, shadows in the darkness, driving the booty of their raid along in front of them.

Proctor stepped out of the doorway and watched them disappear. He shoved his Colt back into his holster and muttered a heartfelt, "Damn!"

Mertz hurried toward the barn while Willie turned

to Antonio and Rico. "You folks all right?" the shotgun
guard asked the shaken father and son.

"Sí, I think so," Antonio said. "Rico, are you hurt?"

Rico shook his head. "No, Papa. But when I saw
that Indian come out of the barn . . ." Rico buried his
face against his father's chest, and Antonio tightened his
arms around the boy.

Mertz came out of the barn and walked slowly
toward the station, his face set in hard lines. As he
came up to Proctor and Willie, he said harshly, "They
killed my hostlers, all three of 'em! Thank God they
didn't have time to work them over!" He passed a hand
over his face, and his shoulders suddenly slumped. He
turned to Antonio and Rico and said, "Reckon we owe
you our lives, son. They'd have moved in on the station
building next. Damn! I should have posted a guard."

"Too late for that now," Proctor said bitterly. "All
the horses are gone except that team of six in the
corral."

"You'll need them for the coach tomorrow."

Willie Morse asked, "What about you, Mr. Mertz?"

"This is my station," Mertz said, his voice expres-
sionless. "I'll stay. When you get to San Angelo, you
tell the line to send me more horses and hostlers."

"You can't stay here by yourself," Willie protested.
"Once we leave in the morning, the Indians will know
you're alone."

"Reckon that's a chance I'll just have to take."

"But—"

Proctor interrupted the shotgun guard by saying,
"It's Mertz's choice, Willie. Let it lay."

Reluctantly, Willie nodded his agreement.

From the back door of the station, Louis Shepherd
asked, "What happened?" He had a small pistol in his
hand, having produced the weapon from an inside pocket
of his coat when the shooting started.

"Indians," Mertz said bitterly. "Killed my hostlers
and run off the stock. You don't have to worry, mister.
They're gone now, and I don't think they'll be back
tonight."

Shepherd nodded and slipped the pistol back into

its holster. He turned around to find Lacey Ellis standing close behind him, with Allen Kerry just behind her.

"I suppose you heard," Shepherd said.

Lacey nodded. "Comanche trouble. It's been a long time coming."

Allen was pale and visibly shaken. "My God," he said in a choked voice, "did that man say some of his helpers had been killed?"

"All of them, I think," Shepherd replied. He looked past Lacey and Allen to the corner where Eleanora waited, her face frozen in fear. Quickly, he strode across the room to her side. "It's all right now," he said softly, reassuringly. "The danger is over."

"D-danger?"

Shepherd nodded gravely. "Indians."

Eleanora closed her eyes, and for a moment Shepherd thought she was going to faint. That would have been all right with him; when it came to swooning ladies, he had more than his share of experience and knew how to turn the situation to his advantage.

Eleanora did not faint, though. Instead, she said in a whisper, "I knew we shouldn't have come out here to this wilderness."

Across the room, Allen was shaking his head. "Savage Indians," he said. "Good Lord, what's next? Desperadoes? Floods? And you profess to love this country, Lacey!"

"I do," Lacey said. "Of course there are risks. Everything worthwhile has its risks."

"But this is ridiculous! At the rate we're going, we'll be lucky to reach your father's ranch alive! I think we should turn around and go back, right now."

Proctor came into the building in time to hear Allen's loud comment, and he growled, "Ain't goin' to be no turnin' around. That stagecoach is goin' ahead, just like it's supposed to."

"But surely there will be another stage coming through, going north," Allen protested.

Proctor shook his head. "Not for another four days. By then, you can be where you're going."

Allen nodded grudgingly. "I suppose you're right."

But it was clear from his expression that he did not like it one bit.

He turned around expecting to see Lacey, but she had moved away from him while he was talking to Proctor. She was over by the wall now, where several rifles hung on wooden pegs.

Allen joined her and asked dubiously, "What are you thinking about, Lacey?"

"Just seeing what kind of hardware Mr. Mertz has on hand, in case there's more trouble." Her eyes scanned the rifles. "Winchesters and Henrys. Good weapons," she mused.

"What are you telling me?" Allen asked. "That if there's an Indian fight, you're going to get one of these guns and be right in the thick of it?"

His voice was angry and accusing, and Lacey responded in kind. "We might need every gun we can get," she said. "Of course, you never even considered grabbing a rifle and helping out. But at least you could load for us!"

She saw the hurt in his eyes, and as soon as the harsh words were out, she wished she could call them back.

"I've never fired a gun in my life," Allen said. "You're right. What good am I?"

Lacey reached out and put a hand on his arm, but he shrugged it off and turned away.

Antonio and Rico came in, Antonio's arm around the boy's shoulder, clutching him tightly as if he was afraid to let him go again. Lacey went over to them and said, "Are you all right, Rico?"

Rico nodded. "*Sí.*" He seemed subdued, as well he might.

"It was my fault," Antonio said. "I should never have let him go out by himself."

"You didn't know there was any Indian trouble," Lacey assured him. She cast a glance at Ben Proctor. "In fact, none of the passengers did. But you didn't seem too surprised, Mr. Proctor."

"You tend to your business, little lady, and I'll tend to mine," Proctor told her, then swung around and stalked out into the night before Lacey could respond.

"You will stay with me all the time from now on," Antonio told Rico. "I do not want you out of my sight."

"Sí, Papa."

Tired, Lacey sank down on one of the benches beside the table. This trip had been difficult enough so far. It looked like it was going to get worse.

Chapter Four

The clouds moved on during the night, and the next day dawned bright and clear. In addition, there was a warm wind out of the south, a welcome change from the day before.

Tucker McCall sat his horse on top of a slight rise, thinking it was a shame for a slaughter to happen on a pretty day like this.

Strange attitude for a buffalo hunter, he thought. He had killed hundreds of the beasts himself over the years, but somehow what he was witnessing now affected him differently. Maybe his musings the day before about the buffalo dying out had changed his mind about the whole thing.

Burl Wayne had led his men into position before sunrise, and as soon as it was light enough to aim, the kill had begun. The men had approached carefully so as not to spook the herd, and their first few volleys had been devastatingly deadly. Dozens of the buffalo had staggered and dropped before the others knew what was going on. Now, the smell of blood filling their nostrils, the herd milled in its fright but did not bolt. That tendency was something the hunters always counted on.

Gradually, the herd did begin to move, but its flight was slow. The hunters kept up easily, having only to change their firing positions occasionally. Once they were situated, they would lie prone on the prairie with the barrels of their Sharps rifles resting on forked stakes driven into the ground, and the withering fire would begin again.

As the herd moved, the skinners began their work on the corpses left behind. Helen drove her wagon over ground dotted with shaggy bodies. When she brought it to a halt, the skinners unhitched the team of mules and used them literally to rip the hides from the buffalo, once a few strategic cuts had been made in the skin. It was bloody work, but men and mules both were used to the smell of death.

The hides were stretched and staked out to dry in the warm sun, and the skinners moved on to the next bunch. It was time for him to move on, too, Tucker thought as he heeled his horse into motion. It did not pay for a scout to stay still too long. Everybody else was busy, and they were relying on him to circle the valley, keeping an eye out for trouble.

The morning was a long one, and by the time the sun was overhead at noon, all the hunters and skinners were tired. They kept going, though, since this might be the last time any of them had a chance at a herd of this size.

The sun was downright hot. Tucker paused again in his rounds to wipe sweat from his forehead and then reached into his saddlebag and brought out a piece of jerky to chew on. He had just set his teeth into it when he saw movement on the low ridge across the valley.

Leaning forward in the saddle, he narrowed his eyes as three horsemen appeared. As soon as he spotted them, they stopped and simply sat there, looking down into the valley where the killing continued unabated. Minutes later, a few more riders showed up. Then more followed, trickling in until a good-sized force was waiting on the ridge.

"Damn," Tucker said softly, then kicked his horse into a gallop.

He knew approximately where Burl Wayne was, and he headed straight there, racing past the staked-out hides, not even glancing at the wagons as he thundered by them. He was vaguely aware that Helen called out to him, but there was no time to acknowledge her.

Tucker spotted Wayne lying on the ground, aiming his Sharps into the milling herd. Wayne's size made him look almost like a boy at play, but there was nothing childish about what was going on here. Tucker yanked the reins and was out of the saddle before the horse came to a complete stop.

He glanced up at the ridge and saw the Indians still sitting there, making no move to attack. It seemed strange that none of the other hunters had noticed them, but then everyone down here in the valley was concentrating on the task at hand. Dropping to one knee beside Wayne, Tucker said, "We've got company."

Wayne fired the Sharps, its butt jerking back forcefully against his shoulder. Out in the herd, a cow jolted, took a couple of steps, and then nosed down into the dirt. Wayne looked up at Tucker and said, "What the hell are you talkin' about?"

Tucker nodded toward the Indians.

Wayne looked in that direction, and his whole body tensed when he saw the ominously waiting force. "Goddamn!" he exclaimed. "That must be the whole Comanche nation up there!"

"Not hardly," Tucker said. "Maybe a hundred or more. Enough that we're in for trouble, though. We'd best get out of here."

Wayne's gaze darted back and forth between the herd and the Indians; he was obviously torn about what to do. Though the group had already killed several hundred of the buffalo, thousands of the animals were still out there, waiting to be slaughtered and skinned. Thousands of buffalo . . . representing thousands of dollars' worth of hides.

Burl Wayne came to his feet and, over the roar of the guns, shouted, "Hold your fire!"

As the gunfire gradually died, Wayne passed the word to stop the hunt. When some of his men asked him why, he waved a hand at the watching Indians. "Let's get movin'!" he called. "Some of you men help the skinners!"

Tucker checked his own Sharps, making sure it was loaded and ready. The Indians stood several hundred yards away, but if they started to charge, Tucker felt sure he could down a few of them even at that range.

The pace became frenzied as the hunters, well aware of the threat, got ready to pull out as fast as possible. Burl Wayne watched the Indians and cursed bitterly. "Look at 'em!" he said. "Just waitin' over there like a bunch of damned vultures! What are they waitin' for, anyway?"

Without taking his eyes off the Comanches, Tucker said, "Reckon they enjoy making us nervous. Besides, they're letting you do all the dirty work for them."

Wayne cast a sidelong glance at him. "What do you mean?"

Tucker jerked a thumb at the rapidly working skinners. "An Indian uses the whole buffalo, not just the skin. But he's willing to let you get the hide off for him, because he knows we can't move very fast with a couple of loaded-down wagons. They'll attack when the skinning's done. I'd wager money on it."

"Sounds like you think we shouldn't be skinnin' those animals."

"Our best chance of getting out of this alive is to leave the wagons and the skins and ride out of here—right now," Tucker said flatly.

Wayne glared at him. "I won't leave those skins," he said angrily. "I've worked too damn hard—for years. Those hides are mine, and I'm not gonna leave them for a bunch of heathen savages to wrap up in!"

"It's your choice," Tucker said with a shrug. "You're in charge of this bunch, and I hired on to take orders."

"Don't you forget it," Wayne growled. He stalked away to hurry the men, tearing into them verbally.

Tucker stayed where he was. He thought he had the Indians figured out, but you could never be absolutely sure how an Indian's mind was going to work. Yet they showed no signs of hostility as the group continued to pack up. There was no time to worry about drying the skins; that could be done later, if there was a later. No doubt they would lose some of the hides to rot, but there was no choice. Speed was what mattered.

The hour after Tucker rode back to the hunt was one of the longest he had ever spent. Finally, though, the hides were loaded and the hunters were mounted,

with the skinners riding their own horses now, and with
Helen at the reins of one wagon and a driver named
Duffy at the other. Tucker rode over to Helen's wagon
and stopped beside it. She smiled at him, her face wan
and frightened. "It's going to be all right, isn't it, Tucker?"
she asked.

"Sure it will," he replied, putting more confidence
in his voice than he actually felt. "We'd stand a better
chance if your brother had left these hides behind,
though."

Helen's mouth quirked. "Burl? Pass up a chance to
make money? You don't know him as well as I do."

"Reckon that's true," Tucker muttered.

"Will you . . . will you stick close by the wagon as
much as you can, Tucker?"

He nodded. "When I can."

"I don't want to be captured. You understand,
don't you?"

Tucker understood. All too well, he understood.
He knew what Comanches did to captive white women.
Death was better, all right.

At last the group was ready to move out. Tucker
waved a hand at Helen and spurred ahead, reining in
when he drew alongside Burl Wayne.

"You're the scout, McCall," Wayne said. "Which
way do we go?"

The original plan had called for the group to return
north once they had the hides. That was impossible
now, since the Indians were waiting in that direction.
"Way I see it, we've got to go south," Tucker said.

"None of us knows that country," Wayne protested.

"We know what's waiting the other way. I think we
ought to make for Adobe Walls. It's somewhere south
of here, and I heard that somebody was putting in a
trading post there. It's our best chance."

Wayne nodded slowly. "Pass the word," he said to
one of the other hunters. "We're headin' south."

With shouted cries, the word was passed, and the
hunters turned their horses toward the south. Helen
and the other wagon driver got ready to whip their

mule teams into motion. Wayne led out, Tucker just behind him.

The men yelled to urge their horses on, and whips popped as the wagons got under way with wheels creaking from the heavy load of hides. The noise of the hunters' departure filled the little valley. From the ridge, the Indians continued to watch in ominous silence.

Tucker looked over his shoulder and saw Helen fighting the reins as the mules dragged the wagon over the rough ground. She swayed back and forth on the box as she hauled on the lines. Tucker turned his horse and rode back, falling into step beside the wagon.

"Need me to drive?" he called to her.

Helen shook her head. "I've wrestled these four lop-eared bastards for hundreds of miles! I'll do all right!"

Tucker grinned at her. He could not help but admire the woman's spirit.

Even over the din that filled the air, Tucker somehow heard faint cries come floating down from the ridge. He felt his heart begin to race as he twisted in the saddle and saw the Comanches begin their attack.

They rolled down the gentle hillside like a wave, scores of warriors riding tough little ponies. Tucker yanked his horse in a circle and bawled out at the top of his lungs, "Here they come!"

Helen used the whip on the mules, urging them on to greater speed, but they could not move much faster than they already were.

Several of the hunters reined up and dropped from their saddles. Their rifles were loaded and ready, and they used their horses for support as they lined up the barrels on the charging Indians. Tucker was among them, talking softly to his horse to keep him calm as he aimed at one of the Indians in the forefront of the charge, a good half a mile away.

He touched the trigger. The Sharps boomed and kicked, smoke pluming from its muzzle and making it impossible to see for a moment. But then the warm breeze out of the south blew the smoke away, and Tucker saw a riderless horse near where he had been aiming, the animal running pell-mell along with the other horses.

At this range, a hit was just as much luck as skill, and Tucker knew it. But several of the Indians were down, a tribute to the hunters' marksmanship.

The first volley did not slow down the charge, and Tucker reloaded hastily, sliding one of the long cartridges from his shell belt into the breech of the Sharps with practiced ease. He brought up the long, heavy barrel and rested it on his saddle again, took a moment to aim, then fired.

By this time so much smoke hung in the air that he could not tell if his shot was true or not. He glanced over his shoulder and saw that the group had moved on. He grabbed the saddle horn and swung up, kicking the horse into a gallop. The other hunters who had hung back to delay the Indians were doing the same. They would catch up with the main body, then dismount and continue fighting their rearguard action. That way the distance between them and the rest of the hunters would not be so great that the Indians could split them into two groups.

Tucker rode hard until he drew even once more with Helen's wagon. He looked over and saw that she was leaning forward on the box, popping the whip, cursing, and driving the mules on with sheer effort of will. She glanced up and met his eyes for an instant; that was all either one of them had time for.

Tucker reined in, flinging himself out of the saddle and raising the Sharps that he had reloaded while catching up to the others. He fired the big rifle and then squinted through the powder smoke, unable quite to believe what he was seeing: The Indians were peeling off, some to the east, some to the west. Slowly, they began to flank the group of buffalo hunters.

He and the others were trapped, Tucker realized. There were just too damn many of the Indians. Riding the fleet ponies, they could easily outdistance the hide-burdened hunters. It was only a matter of time, Tucker knew, until they would be surrounded and wiped out.

But the Indians did not try to encircle them. Once

more Tucker thought there was just no figuring how an Indian's mind worked. It became obvious as the Comanches raced along the flanks of the group that they were content for the moment simply to drive the hunters on. Occasionally a few braves would split off and charge in to exchange shots with the hunters, but they did little damage and seemed intent on harassment rather than murder.

The hot afternoon became an eternity. At one point, Tucker found himself riding next to Burl Wayne, who was cursing bitterly at the Indians.

"Why don't they just get it over with, dammit?" Wayne spat. "They're just playin' with us, the blood-thirsty red devils!"

"You're right," Tucker agreed. "They want to chase us until we drop, then have their fun."

Tucker told himself that when the showdown finally came, he would fight at Helen's side. He would keep his promise to her. Though their relationship had not developed as she had hoped, he did have some feeling for her.

He turned and rode back to her wagon. As he pulled up beside the vehicle, he saw how pale Helen was. Her face was bathed in perspiration, and her shirt was plastered wetly to her body. She was exhausted.

Tucker did not ask her if she wanted him to spell her at the reins; he knew what she would say. Instead, he kicked his feet free of the stirrups and stepped onto the box, keeping hold of the reins of his own horse. Deftly slipping the reins over his horse's head, he tied them to the other side of the wagon to keep the horse running alongside.

"Move over," he said, taking the reins of the wagon from her hands. "I'll drive for a while."

She started to protest but then wearily moved over on the seat. "I'm too tired to argue with you, Tucker," she said.

"Good." He took the whip from her and snaked it out over the backs of the mules, popping it and getting a fresh surge of power from the animals.

"What's going to happen, Tucker? We can't go on much longer."

"Reckon you know the answer to that as well as the rest of us," Tucker replied.

"Yes," Helen said. "I suppose I do. Tucker, I—"

Another burst of shooting drew their attention before Helen could finish what she had started to say. Tucker exclaimed, "Damn!" He slammed his fist on the seat in anger and frustration.

"What is it?" Helen asked.

"Look what they're doing," he told her, pointing. "They're going after the remuda!"

This time a larger group of Indians was racing in, firing at the hunters who were charged with keeping the remuda moving. As Tucker and Helen watched, two of the men fell from their saddles, their bodies riddled with bullets and arrows. The other men abandoned the spare horses, pulling their own mounts around and riding away. The victorious Indians drove the horses away from the fleeing group, their shrill whoops cutting through the air.

"It doesn't really matter, does it?" Helen asked after a moment. "After all, we're not going to need those horses, are we?"

"No," Tucker answered slowly. "I reckon not."

By late afternoon, men and horses were ready to drop in their tracks. On the wagon, Tucker had handed the reins back over to Helen, and now he was pushing his own exhausted mount back up to the front of the group.

Burl Wayne saw him coming and laughed harshly. "We're still alive, ain't we? We still got them hides. I told you I wasn't givin' up, McCall!"

"That's right." Tucker's voice was grim. "You don't really think we're going to get out of this, though, do you?"

"Why the hell not? Maybe those Indians are just as tired as we are."

Tucker opened his mouth to tell Wayne there was

no chance of the Indians giving up, when jubilant shouts from the outskirts of the group distracted him.

One of the hunters used his horse's last reserves of strength to race the animal toward Tucker and Wayne. "They're pullin' out!" he cried. "The goddamned Injuns are leavin'!"

Tucker gaped at the man, thinking that the ordeal had unhinged his mind, but the cry was being taken up by the other men. He looked over at Wayne and saw that he was equally shocked. "Can't be," Tucker muttered to himself. He spurred out ahead to get a better look.

It was true, he saw, astonishment on his face. The Indians on both flanks were curving away from them. As Tucker watched, they began to disappear over the horizon. There was no question that they had decided not to close in on the band of hunters.

Tucker grinned humorlessly. So far, the Indians had done just the opposite of what he had figured. When he thought about it, though, this latest maneuver sent a clear message: The Indians were saying that they could come back at any time and kill the white invaders at their leisure.

"We can't slow down," Tucker said to Burl Wayne. "We've got to keep moving right through the night. The ground's dry enough now that we shouldn't hit any patches that'll bog us down."

Wayne nodded. "I want to put as many miles behind us as we can. Where do you reckon this Adobe Walls place is?"

Tucker considered even as he waved the wagons and the hunters on, urging them to keep up the pace, killing though it was.

"It's down on the Canadian River, if what I heard is right," he said. "Another twenty or thirty miles. If we drive on all night, we might make it by late tomorrow, loaded down like this." Tucker paused. "We could make a lot better time if we left the wagons behind."

Wayne jerked around to face him. "We ain't leavin' those wagons!" he blazed. "I've lost men and run horses into the ground today. I ain't lettin' the Indians have those hides!"

Tucker sighed wearily. He turned his horse around, unwilling to argue with Wayne, not as tired as he was.

"What's happened, Tucker?" Helen asked as he rode up to the wagon. "Is it really true? Have the Indians all left?"

"As best we can tell," Tucker said. "I can't explain it, but I'm grateful for whatever caused it. We can't slow down, though. We've got to take advantage of this chance. There probably won't be another one."

Helen nodded as she bounced on the seat. The stench of the hides behind her filled her nostrils. It had been making her slightly sick to her stomach for the last hour. Her arms and legs felt like lead, and her back was stabbed by pains. But she kept going, drawing strength from these brief conversations with Tucker. He was not giving up; damned if she was going to.

The group hurried on into the late afternoon. Despite their resolve not to slow down, the hellish day was taking its toll. Though the effort was as valiant as ever, the result was not what it had been earlier. Horses and mules were moving slower now, and there was nothing that could be done to speed them up.

A half hour passed as the sun moved closer to the western horizon, casting a reddish glow over the plains. The Indians did not reappear, and Tucker began to feel hope growing in him. He doubted they would attack at night, so if the hunters could elude them for the next hour or so, they would have the whole night in which to get a good lead on the Comanches.

Fate decreed differently. The second wagon was following closely behind Helen's vehicle when one of the lead mules suddenly stumbled, falling and taking down the one next to it, as well. Immediately there was a pileup, mule smashing into mule and the wagon slewing around crazily. A loud cracking noise split the air. The driver yelped and cursed as he was thrown from the seat.

Tucker twisted around in the saddle and saw the accident. "Hold it," he called to Helen, then galloped back to check the damage.

Tucker looked at Wayne in disbelief. "You don't have a spare axle?"

"Things like that cost money." Wayne spat and then shook his head in disgust. "Who could figure that this would happen?"

Tucker stared at Wayne and fought back the urge to pick up the little man and shake him like a dog shakes a rat. There was no end to Wayne's greediness.

"Well, we'll just have to leave the wagon," Tucker finally said. "We can unhitch the good mules, and Duffy can ride one of them."

Wayne's gaze was shocked and angry as he looked at Tucker. "Leave them hides?" he said. "You know better than that, McCall. I ain't leavin' a single goddamned one of 'em behind!"

"What are you going to do, pack them on your back?"

Most of the other hunters had gathered around by this time, and Helen was also watching from her perch on the other wagon. Wayne's face was flushed as he glowered at Tucker and the broken wagon in turn.

"There's got to be some way," Wayne muttered. "There's got to be."

For the first time, Tucker thought about getting on his horse and riding away from here. He had signed on back in Dodge to do a job, not to get killed on account of someone else's stubborn greed. He knew his chances would be just as good on his own, since he could move a lot faster that way.

But Helen was still here, and he did not think she would agree to leave Wayne. Lord knew she had enough cause to ride away from him and never look back, but Tucker just did not believe she would do it.

There were the other hunters to consider, too. Whether he liked them or not, a man did not run out on his partners.

"I told you, McCall, I'll fight the whole damned Comanche nation before I give up them hides," Wayne said.

Tucker just looked at him. "Like I said, you may just have to."

Chapter Five

At the stage-line way station, the three hostlers slain by the Comanches were buried the morning after the surprise attack. Standing with the rest of the group next to the three new graves, Lacey Ellis let the sunshine warm her, but inside she was still cold. The night had been long and chilly, and the funeral had not made anyone feel better.

Now the simple service was over. Stationmaster Mertz had said a few words over the graves that he and Willie Morse had dug at dawn. Then he led them in a short prayer. That was all that could be done for the dead men.

With Allen Kerry beside her, Lacey turned away from the graves with their crude wooden markers, located near a small clump of stubby trees about fifty yards behind the barn, in which the stagecoach was waiting to be hitched up. While Mertz had conducted the service, Willie and Ben Proctor had stationed themselves away from the group, so that they could keep an eye open for trouble. The Indians could possibly return at any moment, and because of this all the men were armed with rifles. Allen looked uncomfortable holding the weapon; Lacey hoped he would not have to use it.

Rico Lopez was very solemn as he walked back toward the station, his father's hand on his shoulder. Antonio had explained to him that no one blamed him for the deaths of the hostlers, that in fact he had probably helped save the lives of everyone else, but still the boy was sad and upset. Lacey could not blame him for that.

Eleanora Morrison was pale and hollow eyed this morning, not having slept much the night before. No one had felt much like sleeping, and the crude accommodations made it that much more difficult. Louis Shepherd hovered near her.

As the group returned to the way station and were rejoined by Proctor and Willie, Lacey turned to Mertz and said, "Why don't you come with us, Mr. Mertz? You can't be serious about staying out here by yourself."

"Somebody's got to," Mertz replied stubbornly, "at least until the company decides to close down this part of the line. And that decision's not up to me."

"I'm sure no one would expect you to—" Allen began.

"Maybe nobody but me," Mertz said. "But if the next coach comes through on schedule, I'll be here to meet it. Maybe I can round up some more horses between now and then, if the company doesn't send out any."

Proctor shook his head, clearly at a loss to understand Mertz's attitude. Yet it was the old fool's own business if he wanted his hair to wind up decorating an Indian's lance.

"You see or hear anything out there, Willie?" Proctor asked his partner.

Willie shook his head. "Not a thing. I thought I saw something moving once in the chaparral, but then I couldn't see it anymore. Could have been an animal or something."

Proctor frowned. Under the circumstances, he did not like anything left unexplained. Willie was no greenhorn, but he did not have enough natural suspicion, either. "Whereabouts was this you saw?" Proctor asked.

Willie started to point to the west of the station. "Over there," he said. "Right about where that bunch of mesquite—"

There was a whistling sound, and then Mertz, who was standing beside Willie, let out a choked, strangling gasp. He staggered, dropping his rifle and grasping feebly at the shaft of the arrow in his throat. Before he could tear it loose, crimson flooded over his fingers; he fell heavily.

Eleanora screamed.

Yelling, half a dozen Comanches sprang up from their place of concealment and ran toward the stunned group of whites. More arrows zipped through the air.

"Into the barn!" Proctor shouted. "Come on!"

Lacey shoved her own fear and panic into the back of her mind and gave Allen a push toward the barn. "Go on!" she rapped at him. Two quick steps took her to Mertz's side. She kept her eyes away from the bloody ruin of his throat as she bent to scoop up his fallen rifle.

She saw that Allen had not moved, and grabbing his arm, she started toward the barn. Proctor and Willie were almost to the barn door, firing their rifles as they ran. Shepherd had hold of Eleanora's arm and was urging her along, much like Lacey was doing with Allen. Antonio Lopez, thankfully, had grabbed up Rico and raced with him through the entrance into the temporary safety of the barn.

No one else was hit during the frantic dash, though arrows were flying around them. Lacey was the last one through the double doors, and as soon as she was clear, Proctor and Willie shoved them closed behind her.

"Cover that other door!" Proctor shouted to Willie, who turned and ran to the opening that led out into the corral. Willie crouched there with one of Mertz's Winchesters, ready to fire at anything that moved. His shotgun was up on the box of the stage, at the center of the barn, but it would not do much good unless the Indians got closer.

There were no windows in the barn, but there were several gun slits, as in the station building itself. Proctor crouched at one of the slits and fired steadily until the Winchester ran out of lead. Lacey appeared at his side, thrusting Mertz's rifle at him and taking the empty one.

Proctor glanced over his shoulder. "Let's get some help up here, you two!" he barked at Allen and Shepherd. Allen moved up gingerly to one of the gun slits and awkwardly poked the muzzle of his rifle through it. Lacey had shown him how to work the lever. He squinted over the sights, not really sure what he was aiming at since there were no Indians in his line of sight at the moment. He made an effort to keep his eyes open, as Lacey had instructed him, and squeezed the trigger.

The blast was deafening, and the recoil slammed against his shoulder with unexpected force. He shook his head, then worked the lever and jacked another shell into the chamber, the ejected casing clattering at his feet.

Louis Shepherd started toward one of the slits, but Eleanora clutched at his arm in desperation. "Don't leave me!" she gasped. "Please! Stay here and protect me!"

Gently, Shepherd disengaged his arm from her grasp. "I've got to help," he told her. "I can do you more good by killing some Indians."

Eleanora seemed not to hear him. Tears welled from her eyes, and her body shook. Shepherd did not want to leave her, not when he had gotten himself into her confidence, but there was no choice. Cultivating a rich widow lady would not do him a damn bit of good unless they got out of there alive.

Not for the first time, he cursed the fate that had led him into this situation. If he had been able to return east, where a man of his talents would be more at home, then he never would have found his life in danger from a bunch of crazed savages. The only thing he could do now, though, was try to save himself and Eleanora.

Proctor was only firing now when he had a good target, which was not often. The Indians would charge forward for a few steps and then dive to the ground. Apparently they had no rifles, but some of them were armed with pistols, and they were using those now instead of their bows and arrows.

While Proctor was waiting to catch sight of another Comanche, Lacey said to him, "We can't stay in here forever. They'll set fire to the place."

"I know," Proctor replied grimly.

"How about hitching up the team and making a break for it in the coach?"

Proctor regarded her with narrowed eyes. "I was thinkin' that same thing. Reckon it's about all we can do." He twisted and called, "Anything movin' back there, Willie?"

"Nothing I can see, Ben," Willie answered.

Proctor grimaced. Willie had not seen the Indians sneaking up on them, either. "Reckon you could round up the team if we cover you?"

Willie glanced out at the six horses milling around the far end of the pole corral. He squinted against the bright sunlight and swallowed nervously. "Reckon I can."

"All right, I'll come cover you." Proctor turned to Lacey and slipped his Colt out of its holster. "Can you handle one of these?"

From his position a few feet away, Allen objected, "You can't expect Lacey to shoot those savages!"

Lacey did not even look at him. She took the pistol from Proctor. The weight of it was reassuring, and the walnut butt, worn smooth with use, felt good in her palm.

"I can handle it," she said.

Proctor nodded and then ran to the back door of the barn, joining Willie Morse. "Good thing we stopped them heathens from bustin' down the corral last night," he said. "If they'd got that team, too, we'd be up the creek now."

Willie leaned his rifle against the wall beside the door. "It'll take me a few minutes to round them up, Ben."

"I'll keep 'em off you best I can, kid."

Willie nodded. He took a deep breath and then suddenly sprinted out of the barn.

Proctor caught a flicker of movement to the right and snapped the rifle to his shoulder. He fired just as one of the Comanches raised himself from the conceal-ment of some mesquite. The slug thudded into the

Indian's chest, spinning him around and dropping him
limply to the ground.

Willie tried to grab the mane of one of the horses,
but the animals were already frightened, and this running man only spooked them worse. Several of them
lunged against the railing of the corral, making it sag
dangerously. Willie knew that if they broke out of the
corral and ran, they would be taking the chance for
survival with them. He stopped trying to grab the
horses and settled for whipping his hat off and waving it
at them while he yelled.

Sure enough, the horses bolted toward the barn,
just as he had hoped. He heard the flat crack of a
six-gun and felt something burn on his forearm. Another of the Indians had come around the barn and was
firing at him. Ben Proctor's rifle blasted again, the shot
missing this time but coming close enough to drive the
Comanche back. Willie ran for the barn in the wake of
the horses.

"Get out of the way!" Proctor yelled as the horses
raced into the barn. He ducked out of the doorway to
avoid being trampled.

Shepherd turned around in time to see one of the
animals heading directly toward Eleanora, who was standing beside the stagecoach. He reacted without thinking,
throwing himself toward her, wrapping an arm around
her waist and bearing her back hard against the coach.
The horse thundered past them, two feet away. If not
for his quick action, Eleanora would have been run
over.

Proctor and Willie had the door to the corral closed
by now, and the horses, seeing that there was no way
out, reared, whinnying shrilly. Immediately Proctor and
Willie went to work to calm the animals, approaching
slowly and talking to them in soothing voices. That left
it up to Lacey, Allen, Antonio, and Shepherd to keep
up a defensive fire against the Indians. They did their
best, but Lacey knew their shots were not inflicting
much damage, if any.

It seemed to take forever, but Proctor and Willie
finally got the team quieted somewhat. The horses were

accustomed to being hitched up to a coach, and as the two men began that procedure, the animals calmed down even more. Proctor and Willie did not usually do this part of the job, so it took them longer to hitch up the team than it would have taken experienced hostlers. But finally the coach was ready to go.

The gunfire was more sporadic now, as the Indians had evidently decided to wait out the occupants of the barn. Proctor scrambled up onto the box and took firm hold of the lines. "Everybody on board!" he called.

Shepherd almost had to pick up Eleanora and put her bodily on the stage, she was still so paralyzed with fear. Nearly being trampled to death had only made her terror worse.

Antonio Lopez hustled Rico on board. The boy was frightened but fairly calm; all during the fighting he had huddled next to a bale of hay close by his father.

Allen and Lacey climbed aboard as Willie took the bar down off the big double doors; a firm push was all that was needed to throw them open. Then he hauled himself to the top of the coach. He put one rifle next to him and rested his leg on it to hold it there. He had another Winchester ready in his fists.

As soon as everyone was on board, Proctor picked up the whip and poised it. Then he paused as several thumps sounded. He smelled smoke then and knew that the Indians were shooting fire arrows onto the roof.

"Hold on!" he yelled, then cracked the whip and whooped at the top of his lungs.

The team lunged forward, all six of the animals straining against the traces. Proctor whipped them mercilessly, driving them forward toward the door. They hesitated for just an instant and then plowed into the doors, throwing them open.

The sun was blinding as the coach lurched out of the barn. Proctor kept flailing the whip and shouting. Willie Morse twisted on the roof of the coach, levering and firing as fast as he could as the Indians leaped up from their hiding places. This desperate escape attempt had caught them by surprise.

Eleanora and Rico were huddled on the floor of the

coach. Lacey crouched next to them, unwilling to go all
the way to the floor; she wanted to know what was
happening, good or bad. Shepherd and Antonio fired
from the windows, while Allen balanced on the center
bench, unsure of what to do.

The stage gathered speed as Proctor urged on the
team. Suddenly, several Indians on horseback appeared
in front of it, and Proctor had to haul on the lines to
send the team in a sharp turn. For a second, the coach
leaned and threatened to go over, but then it righted
itself with a teeth-rattling crash. Willie emptied the
Winchester at the pursuing Indians, dropped it, and
grabbed up the other rifle.

It was impossible to tell how many Indians there
were, but the number seemed smaller now. The hail of
fire from the coach had inflicted some casualties, and
now that the white men were no longer penned up in
the barn, the Comanches were starting to debate the
wisdom of this attack.

As the way station receded in the distance, Lacey
caught a glimpse of Mertz's body lying in the dirt of the
station yard. He had been adamant that he was going to
stay here at his post. It looked like he was right.

Slowly, the firing slacked off. Evidently, this was
only a small group of Indians, perhaps part of the band
that had raided the station the night before, and what
had been sport for them had become dangerous work.
They dropped back, ending the pursuit . . . at least for
the moment. It could well be, Lacey knew, that they
were only returning to the main band to summon their
brothers to join in the hunt.

The stage was rolling east over open ground. There
was no trail here, since the regular route led southwest-
ward from the way station, but that way was closed for
the moment. Willie slid down from the roof onto the
box and wiped his forehead with his sleeve, the sweat
leaving a dark stain on his shirt. "What now, Ben?" he
asked.

"We keep going," Proctor grunted. "When we've
put some distance between us and them Indians, we'll

swing south again, head for the Canadian. Once we get there we can follow the river back to the road."

"If we can get through the Indians, you mean."

Proctor grinned, but there was no pleasure in the expression. "That's a big if, boy," he said. "A mighty big if."

By the middle of the afternoon, Ben Proctor did not know where they were. He would have denied being lost, since he knew they were somewhere east of the stage route, but this was new country to him.

He had turned the team toward the southeast a couple of hours before in hopes of finding the Canadian River. So far, they had not seen any more Indians, but everyone on board the stage knew it was only a matter of time. The Panhandle was swarming with Indians this spring.

"How's that nick of yours?" Proctor asked Willie, breaking a long silence.

Willie held up his bullet-grazed arm. "It's nothing," he said. "Just a little scratch." It was the only injury anyone except Mertz had suffered at the way station. "Where do you reckon we are, Ben?" Willie went on.

Proctor grunted sourly. "Hades. South Hades."

"No, really." Willie grinned. "You think we'll be hittin' the Canadian anytime soon?"

"I hope so. I don't know this country too good."

Proctor suddenly stiffened on the seat and peered west. His squinted eyes narrowed even further in concentration.

"What is it?" Willie asked.

"Listen."

Willie listened, and a moment later he heard what Proctor's keen ears had already picked up. The crackle of gunfire came floating lazily through the hot air. "Sounds like somebody else is in trouble," he said.

"Looks like it, too." Proctor pointed. "See them buzzards?"

The scavengers were almost too far away to be

seen, but Proctor had spotted them pinwheeling high in the sky. They were sure signs of death and destruction.

"What do you think happened?" Willie asked.

"Don't know, but I don't want it happenin' to us." Proctor popped the whip to speed up the horses.

Inside the stage, Lacey braced herself against the seat as they picked up speed. She wondered if more Indians were chasing them, but she realized after a moment that the pace was not breakneck enough for that. She felt sure that more trouble was on the way, though, and she let herself sag against Allen, who was sitting next to her. He reached down and took her hand, and the touch was somehow comforting.

Across from them on the other seat, Eleanora sat with her hands knotted tightly in her lap. Her head was down, her gaze slightly vacant. Up until the time that the stagecoach crossed the border into Texas, she had regarded this trip as an ordeal. Since then, though, it had become a nightmare, a journey through hell.

Louis Shepherd was next to her, his arm around her shoulders in an effort to comfort her. He spoke to her in a low, soothing voice, his words inaudible to the other passengers. Allen Kerry had sent several disapproving looks his way, as if he thought Shepherd was trying to take advantage of Eleanora's fright, but Shepherd was ignoring him.

Rico Lopez, demonstrating the resilience of youth, had bounced back somewhat from the violence he had witnessed in the last twenty-four hours. Now he was taking an interest in the landscape rolling by outside the coach window, and his father was pointing out such things as curious-looking rock formations.

Lacey caught part of what Shepherd was saying to Eleanora. "—won't let anything happen to you," the Bible salesman was telling her. Lacey frowned. She still did not trust Shepherd, though she had to admit that the man had at least tried to carry his share of the fighting so far.

Just as Allen had tried to do his part. Lacey admired him for that. She knew he had to be frightened.

He had never faced anything even remotely resembling this situation before.

She remembered the man at the first way station after they had crossed the Texas border, the tall buffalo hunter in buckskins. He had carried a Sharps Big Fifty, and he had looked as if he knew how to use it. If only he were with them now, Lacey knew she would feel much better.

Up on the box, Ben Proctor muttered, "What the hell?" and pulled on the lines to slow down the team. "You see what I see?" he asked Willie.

They had topped a small rise and were starting down the gradual slope on the other side. Off to the west about a mile away were a group of people on horseback. There were two wagons with them, but both vehicles were stopped, and it looked like there were two animals lying motionless in front of it. The riders were sitting around the wagons, none of them moving.

"Is that that bunch of buffalo hunters we saw yesterday?" Willie asked as he squinted into the glare of the lowering sun.

"Sure as hell looks like it," Proctor replied. "Let's swing over there and find out." Already, he felt a surge of relief washing through him. They were not out of danger yet by any means, but if they could hook up with a bunch like this, numbering over a dozen well-armed men, their chances for survival would start to look a lot better.

Proctor turned the coach toward the group and whipped up the horses. He was surprised to see the hunters, but probably no more surprised than they were to see a stagecoach rolling toward them from out of nowhere.

Tucker McCall watched the stage drawing near and wondered where the hell it had come from. The regular stage route ran west of here, crossing the Canadian and heading due south for San Angelo. At least that was what he had been told. This coach was coming from the east, though.

He recognized the driver and the shotgun guard,

and that deepened his puzzlement. It was the coach they had seen yesterday at the way station, all right, but it had gotten a long way off its course since then.

From beside him, Helen asked, "Isn't that the stage we saw yesterday?"

Tucker nodded. "It sure looks like it."

"What are they doing here?"

"Reckon we'll find out."

Burl Wayne knew what the coach was doing here; it was bailing him out of a mess of trouble. At the sight of the big Concord, Wayne's thin lips pulled back in a wolfish smile. If he had been a religious man, he would have considered it the answer to a prayer.

An idea had suggested itself to him as soon as he had seen the coach, an idea that would put an end to this foolishness about abandoning the broken wagon and its valuable cargo. There was always a way if you looked hard enough . . . and if you did not care too much about who got hurt in the process.

It seemed simple enough to Wayne: All he had to do was get the passengers and their luggage off the stage and load the hides onto it. The broken wagon could be abandoned then without having to leave the hides behind.

Of course, that would leave the coach's passengers stranded out here, but that was their problem. Wayne's first concern was getting those hides somewhere he could sell them.

Ben Proctor hauled back on the lines and worked the brake, bringing the coach to a halt about twenty feet from the wagons. He cuffed his battered black hat back on his head and nodded. "Howdy. You folks havin' trouble?"

Burl Wayne stepped forward and waved a dirty hand at the disabled wagon and the two lifeless mules. "Wagon cracked up," he explained. "Broke the axle, killed one mule, and we had to shoot the other." He grinned. "We didn't expect to see a stage comin' through here."

Proctor spat in the dirt. "Injuns chased us off our route. We're headin' for the Canadian."

"Comanches?" At Proctor's nod of assent, Wayne went on, "We had a little run-in with them ourselves. They're all over this part of the country."

The coach doors opened then, and Allen Kerry stepped out. He frowned in recognition as he saw the buffalo hunters. "What's going on here, Mr. Proctor?"

"We just run into more folks been havin' Indian trouble," Proctor explained.

Lacey stepped out of the coach in time to hear Proctor's answer, and she recognized the buffalo hunters as well. She remembered the little man with the scraggly beard who seemed, incongruously, to be their leader, and she recognized the tall, buckskin-clad man who stood next to a wagon, a woman at his side. The skinner who had started the disturbance at the first way station was also standing near the wagons.

Tucker McCall saw the pretty young woman disembark from the coach, and he felt the same unaccountable reaction he had experienced back at the way station. Her clothes were wrinkled, and her hair had come loose from its bun, falling in waves to her shoulders. She had obviously been through some hardships, but Tucker still thought she was one of the most attractive women he had ever seen.

The other passengers climbed down from the stage, all except for Eleanora Morrison, who kept her eyes down and shook her head when Louis Shepherd asked her if she wanted to stretch her legs. Though they were far from being out of danger, this meeting with the buffalo hunters made all of them feel safer.

Ben Proctor got down from the box and stretched his weary muscles, as did Willie Morse. Gesturing at the wagons, Proctor said to Burl Wayne, "Looks like you took quite a few hides."

"Not as many as I wanted," Wayne replied. "And then the axle on this wagon broke."

Proctor squatted on his heels and rolled a cigarette as he studied the broken axle. "Bad luck, all right," he said as he fired up the smoke.

"You wouldn't happen to have somethin' we could use to repair it, would you?"

Proctor shook his head. "You ain't got a spare axle? That's a shame, then, havin' to leave all them hides behind. You can't stay out here, though, not with the Comanches on the warpath. Say, you fellers headin' south?"

Tucker spoke up. "We figured we'd make for Adobe Walls. There's supposed to be some sort of trading post there."

Proctor nodded. "Heard tell there is. You don't mind if the coach travels along with you for a spell, do you?"

"Not at all," Wayne said. He stepped back slightly, his hand going to the long-barreled Remington holstered at his waist. "The stage is goin', all right, but not the rest of you."

Tucker knew right away what Wayne was planning, the knowledge bursting on him like a revelation, but it took Proctor a moment to understand. Tucker said, "Wayne, you can't—"

And Proctor began, "What the hell—?"

Wayne took another step back and slipped the pistol out of its holster. His back was against the wagon now, and from this position he could cover Tucker as well as Proctor and Willie Morse. He had figured that Tucker McCall might give him trouble.

"You boys stand easy," Wayne snarled. "I'll shoot the first one who moves."

"See here!" Allen exploded. "What's the meaning of this?"

Wayne did not take his eyes off Tucker, Proctor, and Willie as he said, "Shut up, dude. It's simple enough. We're takin' the stage and loadin' the hides on it."

"You can't do that," Louis Shepherd said. "You can't leave us out here."

"The hell I can't." Wayne gestured with the pistol. "You and the guard drop your guns, driver."

Helen stepped up beside her adopted brother as Proctor and Willie reluctantly complied with Wayne's orders. "Burl, you can't mean to abandon these people," she said. "You just can't."

"Keep your damned mouth shut, Helen," Wayne snapped at her. "Get your ass up on your wagon!"

"But Burl—"

Wayne swung his free hand, backhanding her and knocking her off a step. Tucker growled deep in his throat and stepped forward, but Wayne leveled the Remington at him, less worried about Proctor and Willie now that they were disarmed.

"Try it, McCall," Wayne breathed. "Just try to start some trouble. I'd love to put a bullet in your head."

Tucker stopped. He did not doubt for a second that Wayne meant the threat. He glanced around at the other hunters, hoping to see some support. It was like looking at a stone wall. They had moved away from him, isolating him, and he knew that they would back up Wayne in a confrontation. Those buffalo hides meant food and drink to them, and they were not to give them up without a fight.

And it wouldn't do anyone any good, Tucker thought, if he got himself killed now.

Lacey watched the drama with her heart in her throat. The prospect of being abandoned out here on the prairie was bad enough; she did not want to see the big man in buckskins killed on top of that. His actions here and at the way station had proven that he was sympathetic to the stage passengers, unlike the little man called Burl Wayne.

Evidently that sympathy went only so far, though, because Tucker shrugged and said, "All right, Wayne. I don't want to get shot over a bunch of damn buffalo hides."

Wayne smiled thinly. "That's more like it." He glanced at the other hunters, who were watching the scene with rapt attention, and called, "Anybody else got any objections?"

There was silence, a moment that stretched out into several as the other hunters exchanged glances. They all knew what Burl Wayne was like, knew that he would not hesitate to kill anyone who got in his way. Besides, the people on the stagecoach were strangers to them. Nobody owed any allegiances here.

"That's fine," Wayne said. He gestured to a couple of the hide skinners. "Mick, you and Burt get the luggage out of the boot and start loadin' hides, inside and out."

Allen looked at Wayne with outrage plain on his face and said, "You can't get away with this."

"Just watch me." Wayne chuckled.

As Wayne covered Proctor and the others with the big Remington, the buffalo hunters dismounted and began to help with the transfer of the hides. Some of them looked a bit sheepish at what they were doing, but Tucker McCall was the only one who stood apart.

Inside, Tucker was seething. What Wayne was doing was a crime, plain and simple, and he was going to do whatever he could to stop it. At the moment, though, he could not do much of anything. He was no fast-draw artist. By the time he could wrestle out the Colt at his hip, Wayne would have put a hole in him. He considered going for his bowie; he was quicker with it than with a handgun. But if he missed, he would not have another chance, and then the passengers would not have anyone on their side except Helen, and Wayne had her cowed.

One of the hunters jerked open the coach door and then stopped short. He turned his head and called to Wayne, "Hell, there's another woman in here!"

"Well, drag her out," Wayne replied. "I want that coach stuffed full of hides."

The hunter reached into the coach and grabbed Eleanora's arm. She let out a scream as the man brutally pulled her from the coach.

Allen's face went white with rage. "Damn you!" he grated. He started toward the hunter, his fists clenched.

Before he could get there, the skinner called Mick came from behind the coach and got in his way. With a savage grin on his face, Mick grabbed Allen's shoulder, shoved him back, and then sank a fist in his stomach. Allen gasped, doubling over. Another shove from Mick sent Allen sprawling on the ground.

Lacey was at Allen's side in an instant. "You leave him alone!" she yelled at Mick.

He laughed. "I remember you, pretty lady. You cost me a bath in the mud." Mick shot a venom-filled glance at Tucker as he spoke.

Tucker's hands were clenched into fists, and he fought the urge to smash one of them into Mick's ugly face. Instead, he stepped forward slowly and reached down to take Allen Kerry's arm. As he lifted Allen to his feet, he said to Lacey and the other passengers, "Just cooperate, folks. It'll go easier that way."

But the time would come, Tucker promised himself, when things would be different. The time would come.

Louis Shepherd stood by, feeling helpless, as Allen and Lacey tried to comfort the distraught Eleanora. He should have been doing that. He should have stepped up to defend her. Instead, he had hesitated, and if they got out of this predicament alive, she might remember his inaction.

"What the hell is this?" asked one of the skinners who was cleaning out the luggage boot. He had Shepherd's sample case in his hand. "Heavy son of a bitch, whatever it is!"

Shepherd raised a hand. "Please. Those are my Bibles. I'm a Bible salesman."

The hunter rubbed his grizzled jaw. "The Good Book, eh? Not worth much out here, mister."

He tossed the case over his shoulder. The catch sprang open when it landed, and Bibles fell out to scatter over the ground.

"Quit your foolin' around!" Wayne ordered sharply. "We've got to get moving before them Comanches come back."

"They won't be back tonight," Tucker said. He nodded at the sun, which was just about to slip behind the western horizon. "I'd wager that we're safe until morning."

"By mornin' I want to be a long way from here. Get to work on them damn hides!"

As the hunters loaded the hides into the coach, the passengers stood and watched, looking forlorn. After several minutes Antonio Lopez spoke up, his arm tightly around Rico's shoulders. "Señor, you are going to take the coach and leave us behind, no?"

"I'm gonna take the coach, yes," Wayne said impatiently. "I don't care what the rest of you do, greaser."

"How about letting them come along with us on foot, then?" Tucker suddenly asked. "We can't move very fast, not with this many hides. They could stay pretty close, and there would be that many more hands in case of trouble."

Several of the hunters nearby muttered their agreement with Tucker's logic.

"All right," Wayne said after a moment. "You pilgrims can hoof it if you want. I ain't sharin' our food and water with you, though."

"You're still settin' us up to die, mister," Proctor growled.

"You want to take your chances, you can head out down the trail right now, old-timer," Wayne said.

Proctor sighed. "No, I reckon it'd be better if we trailed along after your bunch." His eyes narrowed. "I hope to meet up with you some other time, though."

Wayne ignored the implied threat and returned his attention to the transfer of the hides from the wagon to the coach. Several men were stuffing buffalo hides into the coach while others passed hides up to men on the box. They were piled high on the top of the coach. The luggage boot was already full.

Fifteen minutes later, Mick dusted off his hands and said to Wayne, "Reckon that's all she'll hold."

Wayne looked at the coach. It was crammed full, every available inch stuffed with hides. "All right," he said. "Now get mounted, you men! Duffy, you've driven coaches before, haven't you?"

Before the skinner could answer, Ben Proctor stepped forward and declared, "I'll drive her for you." The passengers looked at him angrily, considering this an act of betrayal, but Proctor stolidly ignored them.

Wayne considered for a moment, then said, "I don't think so, old man. I don't trust you—but I do trust Duffy, and if I'm not mistaken, he used to drive stages for a livin' till I recruited him to drive one of the wagons. Besides, hadn't you ought to stay with your charges here?" Wayne grinned arrogantly.

Following Wayne's orders, Duffy climbed up on the box and picked up the whip. Wayne was ready to shout the order to move out when he realized that Helen was standing beside him again. "What is it now?" he asked her.

Helen's thin face was determined as she said, "I want the women and that little boy to ride on the wagon with me, and I think you should let the men take turns on the two extra mules."

"That wagon don't need any more weight, and I'm saving those mules for when we need 'em," Wayne said stubbornly. "Now get goin'."

"No, Burl."

Wayne had been turning away from her in dismissal, but he stopped and stared at her in surprise. Defiance wasn't something he expected of her.

"I mean it, Burl," Helen went on firmly. "Otherwise I'm going to dump some of those hides and make room for everybody to ride."

"The hell you say," Wayne exclaimed.

Helen smiled thinly. "I don't think your men are going to shoot a woman, Burl, especially not after all I've done for them." A touch of bitterness tinged her voice.

After a moment Wayne muttered, "All right. The women and the kid can ride on the wagon, and the others can take turns on the good mule. Not the lame one, though. That'd ruin it for sure. Now get movin', dammit." He supposed it was a small enough concession to make, though he hated giving in at any time. But he didn't want some muleheaded female throwing a fit, and it was true that the extra guns might be needed later.

Helen went over to the passengers and gave them the news. Eleanora was too shaken to respond with anything but a nod, but Lacey shook her head and declared, "Not me. If the others walk, so do I."

"No, Lacey," Allen said, taking her arm. "I insist that you ride."

"But Allen—"

"Please. I won't worry about you nearly as much."

Finally, she nodded. "All right. If that's what you want."

"It is," Allen assured her. Then he turned to Helen. "Thank you so much for standing up for us."

Helen blushed slightly and turned away, starting back for her wagon.

"Just a moment," Lacey called after her. As Helen looked back, she continued, "There's something I've got to do before we take off. Can you wait for a minute?"

Helen looked nervously at Wayne, her brief outbreak of courage starting to wear off now. "Just for a minute," she said.

Lacey hurried over to where the hunters had strewn the unloaded luggage. Most of the bags had popped open, scattering the clothes inside. Lacey rummaged through her belongings and came up with a shirt, jeans, and a pair of boots. "I can't abide this dress any longer," she said to Allen, who had joined her in the ruins of their luggage. "I'm going in that bunch of mesquite over there and change."

"Dammit, what's the holdup?" Wayne yelled over at them.

"You go ahead, Lacey," Allen told her. He turned his back to her as she hurried into the brush, and his glower in Wayne's direction showed how much he despised the little buffalo hunter.

Tucker had swung up onto his horse when all the other men mounted up, and he was watching the proceedings with an ironic smile. It had been good to see Helen stand up to her bullying brother, and it was good now to see the young woman called Lacey doing the same thing.

Lacey . . . An unusual name, Tucker thought, but a pretty one. It suited her.

At that moment, Lacey pushed the brush aside and emerged. Tucker was surprised at the change in her appearance, and judging from the expression on Allen's face, he was, too.

The fancy dress was gone, range clothes in its

place, and Lacey suddenly looked more at home than she ever had in an expensive frock. The jeans were tight, but they had to be in this country, since baggy pants could catch on brush and tear. The man's shirt fit her fairly well and did little to conceal the curves of her firm young body. She had brushed her fingers through her brunette hair, ridding it of the last vestiges of its Boston styling.

All in all, Tucker thought she was more beautiful than ever.

"All right," Lacey said. "I'm ready to go on."

She joined Eleanora and Rico in climbing onto Helen's wagon. There was only room for one person on the seat beside Helen, and Lacey insisted that Eleanora take that place. Rico was upset about being separated from his father, but Lacey calmed him down by promising to keep him company. The two of them settled down on the massive pile of hides in the rear of the wagon. The smell from the uncured hides was awful, but it was the price they had to pay for riding. The hides were vermin-infested, as well, as Lacey quickly found out.

The men were going to draw lots to determine who would ride the mule first. Before the drawing could be carried out, though, Ben Proctor suddenly declared, "The Mex ain't got no part in this. He can walk the whole way."

Antonio's face flushed in anger, but before he could speak, Allen said hotly, "That's not fair. You've gone out of your way to make things harder for this man, Mr. Proctor."

"I'll take turns with white men, but not with a greaser." Proctor sneered.

Allen tensed, ready for the trouble that he knew would come. But his sense of justice had been outraged, and he would no longer back down.

"What the hell's the holdup?" Burl Wayne demanded as he reined up nearby.

"Mr. Proctor doesn't want Antonio to have a turn on the mule," Allen said.

"That damned greaser—" Proctor began.

Wayne cut him off by putting his hand on his gun butt and saying, "I don't like greasers no better'n you, Proctor, but we ain't got time to argue about it. Now draw your damned lots, all of you."

As the luck of the draw had it, Proctor won the privilege of being first on the mule, followed by Allen, Willie Morse, Antonio, and Louis Shepherd.

Helen climbed onto the seat of the wagon and glanced at Allen Kerry, remembering the way he had just stood up to Proctor's bigotry. There was a lot more to that Easterner than first met the eye, she thought as she regarded the young man from Boston.

Burl Wayne shouted the order to move out, and the rude caravan got under way. Eleanora sat huddled on the seat of the wagon, her heretofore tender ears assaulted by the language that poured out of Helen's mouth. Cursing was second nature to Helen while driving the mules, and she could not seem to tone it down.

As the wagon lurched into motion, Lacey slipped a hand down to her waistband. She had purposely left the tails of her shirt out to hide the other item she had secretly taken from her luggage. The hard edges of the Colt pressing into her skin were painful, but it was a welcome pain. If there were more trouble, she would be able to defend herself.

And if the worst came to pass, she would have two bullets: one for Eleanora . . . and one for herself.

Chapter Six

Night fell quickly once the sun was below the horizon, and the warmth of the day vanished with the sun. The night wind was chilly, though not as cold as it had been the previous night.

Burl Wayne pushed everyone hard, riding back and forth along the group and hurrying them along. But no matter how impatient he got, the wagon and the coach could go only so fast.

At first, the group on foot kept up fairly well. Allen, Shepherd, Willie, and Antonio started out walking beside the wagon, with Proctor riding on the mule nearby. It was rough going, though, especially as darkness closed in and they could no longer see the rocks, cactus, and prairie dog holes, which began to slow them down. The pace was especially difficult for Allen Kerry and Louis Shepherd, since they were not accustomed to such grueling physical activity. The other two men had lived in the West all their lives and had led active existences. But all four of the men were well aware that to fall too far behind might cost them their lives, and that made keeping up a more attractive alternative.

With Duffy on the driver's box, the stagecoach pulled out in front of the wagon. Several of the hunters rode on ahead, while others flanked the two vehicles and kept an eye on Helen to make sure she didn't carry out her threat to dump the hides. Bringing up the rear were a few more hunters who kept an eye on the back trail.

It was hard to relax on the bouncing, swaying wagon, but Lacey tried to force herself. She talked to Rico, asking him about the life he and his father had planned once they reached San Antonio. Rico was looking forward to meeting all his cousins, but at the same time he was nervous about it. The ranch where he had been raised was isolated, and he had been the only child there, making him that much closer to his mother. Her death, consequently, had hit him that much harder. Lacey steered the conversation to another topic by telling him about her father's ranch and the vacations she had spent there when she was a little girl.

Up on the bench seat, Helen could not help but overhear some of the conversation between Lacey and Rico. She had to concentrate on her driving, but some of the words stuck with her, and as Lacey and Rico continued to talk about their childhoods, she thought back to her own.

She barely remembered her own parents. Most of her memories centered around the hardscrabble farm owned by Burl Wayne's parents. Life there had been strictly hand to mouth, and she had early on grown accustomed to hardships.

She had also gotten used to letting Wayne do whatever he wanted, since otherwise she got hurt. Even as a boy, Wayne had burned with a desire to have all the things he did not have. And he had learned that to get what he wanted, other people sometimes had to be stepped on.

Soon Helen noticed that Lacey and Rico had stopped talking. In the relative silence she noted that throughout the night Eleanora had said nothing. But then Helen had done nothing to draw her out.

After an hour or so, Rico started to doze off. He had been through a great deal, as all of them had, and weariness made his eyes begin to droop. Lacey slipped an arm around him and let him rest his head on her shoulder. In a few minutes, his deep, regular breathing told her that he was asleep.

Lacey waited a few minutes, until she was sure he was sleeping soundly, then slipped her shoulder from under him and let him snuggle down into the hides. It was a horrible place to sleep, but exhaustion made a better bed of it.

Helen glanced over her shoulder. "Your friend's asleep, too," she said, nodding at Eleanora, whose chin had dipped far down on her chest.

Lacey stepped up to the seat and, putting her hands under Eleanora's shoulders, gently eased her off the seat and back onto the hides. The ordeal had totally drained the older woman, and she barely stirred as Lacey settled her down. Then Lacey climbed up onto the seat next to Helen.

"Don't you want to sleep, too?" Helen asked her.

Lacey shook her head. "Not right now. So much has gone on that I'm not sleepy." She stuck out her hand. "My name's Lacey Ellis."

Helen hesitated a moment and then gathered the reins in her left hand and used her right to shake Lacey's hand. "Helen Wayne. Wish we'd met under better circumstances."

"Me, too," Lacey said dryly. "Like back there at that way station up by the border?"

Helen chuckled. "You mean where Tucker threw ol' Mick in the mud? Served that ugly bastard right."

"Tucker? Is that the other man's name?"

"Tucker McCall," Helen answered. "He's our scout, and a damn good one. He found the herd we took the hides from."

Lacey wrinkled her nose. She had been breathing through her mouth as much as possible to avoid smelling the hides, but the stink did not seem to bother Helen. "Have you been doing this for long?"

"Driving a hide wagon? All my life, seems like. I started when my brother started hunting buffalo."

"Which one is your brother? Or is he even along on this hunt?"

"He's along, all right. He's the one who stole your coach from you. His name's Burl Wayne."

Lacey tried to repress a shudder. "He's your brother?"

"Not by blood. His folks and mine had farms next

to each other. When my parents died, his took me in and raised me as one of their own. So I guess you'd say Burl's my adopted brother."

"That was nice of them, to take you in like that."

Helen snorted. "Got 'em another hand to work the fields, it did. And somebody else for Burl to boss around."

Obviously, it had been a hard life for her, with the pain she had experienced etched in the lines of her face. Lacey knew it was probably none of her business, but she asked, "Why do you stay with him?"

Helen shrugged. "What else am I gonna do? I'm not smart enough to do anything else. Never had any schooling. I can drive a wagon, and I can pleasure a man some. I'd rather be doing them things out here in the open than in some damn brothel."

Even though Lacey believed in being plainspoken, she was a little surprised at Helen's blunt assessment of her life. She supposed it was too much to expect these rough buffalo hunters to allow a woman to accompany them without taking their pleasure from her at night.

Suddenly, she found herself wondering if Tucker McCall had ever visited Helen's blankets. That was none of her concern, she told herself. Where Tucker McCall found his pleasure was none of her business.

Almost as if Helen had read her mind, she said, "Of course, it's gotten some better this trip, what with Tucker being along. He's pretty nice to me."

"I'm sure he is," Lacey said, her voice subdued.

"What about you, Lacey?" Helen asked. "I saw how you were dressed back at that way station. Sure as hell didn't look like you belonged out here then. Now you do, though."

"I was on my way to visit my father. He has a ranch out here."

"Heard you and the boy talking about that. Your pa have a good spread?"

"One of the best, I think. I come to visit him as often as I can. Normally, though, I live in Boston with my mother."

"Your folks split up, huh?"

Lacey nodded. "My mother couldn't stand living in Texas. I've always loved it, myself."

"Haven't seen that much of it. But what I have seen ain't been too impressive," Helen said with a shake of her head.

"The place grows on you," Lacey said, her voice wistful. "Someday, when there's no more Indian trouble, this is going to be a fine place to live."

"Don't reckon I'll ever see it. The buffalo will be gone by then. I don't know what Burl and I'll do then."

"Have you ever thought about trying to go to school someplace, so that you could find something else to do with your life?"

Helen smiled. "Reckon I dream. We all do, don't we?"

"Yes," Lacey said. "I suppose we do."

The two women fell silent for a moment, a silence broken when Helen shouted curses at the mules and popped the whip above their heads. The conversation had given both of them things to think about.

Up ahead, Tucker McCall rode with his face set in taut lines. He was well aware that Burl Wayne was keeping an eye on him and knew that Wayne would not hesitate to shoot him if he did anything Wayne regarded as a threat.

Tucker had hung back long enough to see that the stage passengers were keeping up as well as could be expected, and then he galloped ahead. As long as the Indians were on the prowl, they all were in danger, and the best thing he could do for the passengers was to make sure the group did not head right into trouble.

There was still a bright core of anger burning in him. He did not like anybody pulling a gun on him, especially not a weasel like Burl Wayne. A quick, humorless grin touched Tucker's features. Some of the men called their leader "Weasel" Wayne . . . but not to his face. It was a name that fit.

Tucker pondered the idea of leading a mutiny against Wayne. He knew there was no great loyalty among the men; Wayne ruled them through fear more than anything else. But if he did successfully cross Wayne, he would have to kill the little man. Either that or look over his shoulder for the rest of his life.

Wayne was not the type to forget anything, especially if it cost him money. He would track down anyone who took money out of his pocket and kill him.

Tucker wondered how much of his anger toward Wayne sprang from the fact that Wayne had put Lacey Ellis in danger. He found himself reconstructing her face in his mind. He could imagine what it would feel like to touch the soft skin of her cheek, to smell the fresh fragrance of her hair. There was no wedding band on her finger, so he figured she was not married to that man traveling with her, but she did wear an engagement ring. Tucker knew the fancy-dressed man had to be her intended. An unmistakable surge of envy touched him.

If things had gone differently in his life, if he had been able to continue his education . . . well, there was no telling where he might have wound up. He might have even had a chance with a beautiful young woman like this. As it was, though, he was more suited to a woman like Helen Wayne.

He realized that someone was riding beside him and looked over to see Burl Wayne. "Seen any sign of Indians?" Wayne asked.

"Can't see much of anything in the dark," Tucker replied. "I can tell from the stars that we're still headed southwest, but that's about all I know."

"Well, keep your eyes peeled," Wayne ordered. "And don't think I'm not watchin' you, McCall. I know you'd like to carve me up with that bowie of yours."

"You can rest easy, Wayne," Tucker said flatly. "We got other things to worry about right now. When I get ready to come after you, I'll let you know."

Wayne laughed harshly. "You do that, McCall." He turned his horse and spurred back along the line, looking for anyone who might be lagging unnecessarily.

The stars wheeled through the clear sky overhead, and the group pushed on. Those riding on the wagon, the coach, and on horseback were able to keep up a fair

pace, though the darkness slowed them down somewhat, but the four men on foot continued gradually to
fall behind.

All of them had sore feet by now. Allen's shoes
were not made for walking, and neither were the boots
worn by the other men. None of them were accustomed to walking for any great distance. Back east, a
man took his own carriage or hired a cab if he wanted to
go anywhere, and here in Texas, no man was ever far
from his horse—and no man walked when he could
ride.

As rough as the ride turned out to be, Allen was
glad when his turn on the mule came—and sorry when
it was over.

As the sky began to gray with the approach of
dawn, there were five pairs of blistered feet and leaden
legs. But they had made it through the night without
trouble from the Indians, and that was something for
which to be very thankful.

Tucker left the front and rode back to join Burl
Wayne. He put his horse into a walk next to Wayne's
mount and said, "Reckon we'd better call a halt and let
everybody rest for a few minutes."

"I don't want to stop less'n we have to," Wayne
growled in reply.

"If those horses and mules don't get some food and
water, they can't keep going all day," Tucker pointed
out. "Could say the same thing for the men and the
ladies."

Wayne rasped a hand over his jaw and slowly
nodded. "Could be you're right," he grudgingly admitted. "What do you think about them Indians leavin' us
alone all night like that?"

Tucker grinned. "I've got a feeling there's so many
of them around here it doesn't really matter. They
know they can come after us again anytime they want.
If they'll hold off a couple of days more, though, we
ought to be able to make it to Adobe Walls."

"Think they'll hold off like that?"

A snort of doubt was Tucker's only answer.

Wayne rode along beside the group and called out

for them to halt. Gratefully, men and animals paused to catch their breath and recover some of their strength.

Helen hauled up on the lines and brought the mules to a stop. She stretched and rubbed the small of her back. "Lordy, I'm tired," she said.

"When we start up again, how about letting me handle the team for a while?" Lacey asked.

Helen looked at her in surprise. "You think you could handle a team like this?"

"I told you I grew up on a ranch. I can handle them," Lacey said confidently.

Eleanora and Rico roused from their sleep now that the wagon wasn't moving anymore. Eleanora, looking around at the hides where she had spent the night, was appalled. "I slept *here*?" she wailed.

"Didn't seem to bother you too much last night," Helen said.

Rico hopped down from the wagon and looked around for his father. Lacey had already located the trailing group of men about a hundred yards behind the wagon. "Come on, Rico," she said to the boy. "Let's go meet your father."

The two of them walked back to meet the men, and as Lacey drew near them, she was shocked at how haggard they looked. Of course, everyone was tired—nobody but Rico and Eleanora had slept the night before—but these five looked even worse. Lacey's heart went out to her fiancé, who was limping badly.

"Oh, Allen," she said, taking his arm and letting him support some of his weight on her, "this is awful. That man can't make you go on like this!"

Allen was pale and breathing heavily. "I'd say . . . he can do whatever he wants," he gasped out. "He's got the guns . . . to back him up. That's . . . that's all that matters . . . out here."

Louis Shepherd was finishing his turn on the mule. He slid off the animal's bare back and asked Lacey, "How is Eleanora?"

She frowned, still distrustful of him, but his question seemed sincere. Maybe he was honestly concerned. "She's upset, naturally enough," Lacey said. "But she got some sleep last night. She's no worse off than the rest of us, and better than some."

The stars were disappearing now as the sky became lighter. In a half hour or so, the sun would be peeking over the horizon.

Antonio had scooped up Rico when the boy ran to meet him, and he was still carrying his son. Rico told him how nice Lacey had been to him, and Antonio looked gratefully at the young woman. It was lucky for them that her path had crossed theirs, he thought.

Ben Proctor and Willie Morse walked side by side, but there had been little conversation between them during the night. Proctor, furious at having his stagecoach stolen from him, had spent most of the time planning his revenge on Burl Wayne. He was confident that his opportunity would come sooner or later.

The group on foot soon caught up to the others. Wayne had ordered that no fires be started, so the hunters were making do with a meal of jerky and hardtack, washed down with water from their canteens. The water barrel on Helen's wagon was not empty yet, but it was low enough that it would need refilling the next time they came to a creek. The horses and mules stood with heads down, wearily cropping at the sparse grass and weeds. Two of the hunters got grain for them from bags carried on a packhorse.

Despite what Wayne had said the night before about not sharing supplies with the stagecoach passengers, as the foot-sore group came up to the wagon, Helen handed them some food and passed a canteen among them. "Go easy on the water," she cautioned them. "We don't know this country. There's no telling when we'll be able to refill the barrel."

Allen Kerry slumped to the ground and leaned back against one of the wagon wheels. He stretched his legs out in front of him and looked at his feet. His ankles were swollen around his shoes, and he knew that if he took the shoes off, he would never be able to get them back on. Tearing off a piece of the jerky with his teeth, he found that it almost took too much energy to chew it.

Lacey sat beside him, leaning her head against his shoulder. "I've decided something," she said. "You're going to take my place on the wagon today. I'll walk."

Allen shook his head. "No," he said, his voice a hoarse whisper. "You stay on the wagon."

"But Allen, I don't mind—"

"You're going to ride," he said firmly. "My turn on the mule is coming up soon."

A pair of booted feet stopped beside them, and an unpleasant voice said, "If you want the lady to ride, mister, she can double up with me in the saddle."

Lacey glanced up and saw the hide skinner called Mick standing over them with a leer on his face. "I'd rather walk," she said curtly.

Mick's arrogant grin got wider. "Plenty of room for two. And if you got tired, we could stop and spread out one of them hides from the coach, curl up in it for a little while." He reached down to touch her hair. "Reckon you'd like that, pretty thing?"

Lacey shrunk away from his touch. "I'd rather curl up with the buffalo itself."

Mick's fingers, still close to her head, tangled in her hair and jerked her head up. "Is that so?" he growled.

Moving faster than he had any right to be able to, Allen surged to his feet, bumping Mick with his shoulder. "Let her alone!" he snapped. "You bastard!"

Mick released his hold on Lacey's hair, letting her drop back against the wagon wheel. She put a hand to her head where the hair had been jerked painfully.

Mick glared at Allen and growled menacingly, "Stay out of it, you fancy son of a bitch!"

"You leave this woman alone," Allen shot back at him.

Lacey started to her feet, afraid for Allen. "It's all right—" she began to say, but then Mick reached for her again, and Allen launched a clumsy punch at the skinner's head.

Mick ducked the blow and gave an ugly laugh. "You called the tune, mister," he grated. Then he slammed his fist into Allen's stomach.

Allen gasped and started to double over, but Mick did not give him a chance. The skinner struck again, his knobby fist catching Allen on the jaw and driving him back to go sprawling on the ground. Allen clawed feebly at the dirt but could not pull himself to his feet.

"Leave him alone!" Lacey shouted at Mick. She fought the urge to yank out the hidden Colt and blow off the skinner's loathsome face. She did not want to reveal the gun unless she had to, though, to save Allen's life.

Mick's arm swept out as Lacey got between him and Allen. She staggered back from the shove as Mick slipped his skinning knife from his belt. "I think I'll take your yellow hide, mister," he said.

He had only taken a step when a big hand came down on his shoulder and spun him around. Tucker McCall had suddenly appeared behind the enraged skinner, and now he put all of his strength into a sledgehammer blow that crashed into Mick's jaw. Mick flew backward and bounced off the wagon, but somehow as he fell to the ground, he managed to keep hold of the knife.

A low groan came from Mick as he pushed himself up to all fours. He shook his head to clear it, then looked up at Tucker with murder in his eyes.

Tucker saw the look and said quietly, "Don't do it, Mick. Just leave it be."

"I already owed you, McCall," Mick said, his voice thick. His jaw was broken, and the pain and rage had driven him over the brink into a killing frenzy. He exploded up out of his crouch with a yell.

Tucker moved to the side, letting the maddened skinner brush past him. The keen knife missed by inches. Tucker clasped his hands together and clubbed them down on Mick's back, driving the man facedown onto the ground again.

Mick did not seem to be feeling the pain as he rolled, came back to his feet, and lunged again.

The other hunters were gathered around to watch the fight, whooping and cheering. Forgotten for the moment was the danger all of them were in as they got caught up in this desperate battle.

Lacey knelt beside Allen, holding his head in her lap. He was slowly regaining his senses, though he was still pretty groggy. Close by, Helen Wayne watched intently, her face tight and fearful. She knew how crazy Mick was, knew he would not hesitate to kill Tucker.

Tucker pivoted again as Mick charged at him. He caught Mick's arm and used the man's own momentum against him, swinging him around and letting him go so that Mick plowed into the wagon once more. His face smashed against the frame of the wagon, and when he staggered back, his nose was pulped and leaking blood all over the lower half of his face. He howled in pain, dropping the knife and lurching against one of the horses tied nearby. The hunter who owned the horse had left his Winchester in the saddle boot, and Mick's fingers fell on the stock. His eyes gleamed wildly as he started to drag out the weapon.

"Don't do it, Mick!" Tucker shouted.

The skinner ignored him, yanking the rifle free and spinning around as he levered a shell into the chamber. With another wild yell, he started to lift the Winchester to his shoulder.

Tucker palmed the big bowie from the sheath at his hip and flicked it using little more than his wrist. It took a strong man, and one who had practiced for long hours, to make that throw.

The knife thumped into Mick's chest. He screamed and triggered the rifle, but the shot went wild. He dropped the gun and clawed futilely at the blade buried in his body. The camp was utterly silent, all cheering stilled, as Mick swayed for long seconds and then toppled, dead when he hit the ground.

Breathing heavily from reaction more than exertion, Tucker looked at the body and then glanced over to see Burl Wayne holding the Remington trained on him. "I told him to leave that gun alone," Tucker said.

"I heard you," Wayne admitted. "Mick never did think straight when he got his back up. You just cut our force down by one, McCall."

"Then it wouldn't make sense to shoot me and lose one more, would it?"

After a moment, Wayne carefully let down the hammer of the pistol and shoved it back in its holster. "What can I say? Reckon it was a fair fight." He turned to the other hunters. "What the hell are the rest of you gawkin' at? Standin' around ain't gonna get us away from them Comanches. Get ready to move out!"

As the hunters moved away from the wagon and began preparing to ride again, Lacey helped Allen to his feet. Helen, Eleanora, and Antonio gathered around to make sure he was all right.

Tucker strode over to where Mick's body lay and bent to pull his knife free. He wiped the blade on Mick's dirty jacket and then slid it back into its sheath.

Lacey glanced over at him. "Isn't somebody going to bury that man?"

Tucker shook his head and said, "No time. Besides, I'm not sure he rates a funeral."

Lacey was surprised by Tucker's seemingly callous attitude, but then she told herself that after all, Mick had tried to kill him. Given the circumstances, they could not afford to waste much sympathy on the dead skinner.

Lacey had her hand on Allen's arm. He shook loose from her and strode over to Tucker, his steps slightly shaky. "I suppose I should thank you for saving my life," he said. "That lunatic would have killed me."

"More'n likely," Tucker said.

"Still, you seem to keep fighting my battles for me. I don't want that." Allen's voice was sharp and angry now.

Tucker cast a level gaze at him. "All right. Next time I'll stand by and let you get carved up into little chunks. How's that sound?" He turned back to his horse and started checking his saddle.

"Damn you!" Allen grabbed his shoulder. "All you roughnecks are alike! All you think about is force and killing!"

Tucker held a tight rein on his temper. He did not like people laying hands on him, but this Easterner was

the type who did not know better. He looked over at
Lacey and drawled softly, "Ma'am, you'd best tend to
your friend."

"Friend!" Allen exclaimed. "I'm going to marry
that woman!"

"Best of luck." Tucker shrugged out of Allen's inef-
fectual clasp and stepped up into the saddle, kneeing
the horse into motion before any more could be said.

Lacey said, "Come back to the wagon, Allen. We're
going to be leaving in just a few minutes, and you need
to eat some more."

Allen stared for a moment at Tucker's broad back,
then turned toward the wagon, going along with Lacey's
urging. His face was bleak and set.

"I guess I'm not much of a man," he muttered. "At
least not according to western standards."

"You're a fine man," Lacey assured him. Again,
she laid her hand on his arm.

He pulled away. "You'd rather I was like him."

Lacey bit her lip and wondered what to say. He
was so bitter now; he had been through so much. She
did not know what to do to comfort him.

She stood and watched Allen stalk back to the
wagon. She wanted to call after him, to tell him he was
wrong. Instead, she said nothing.

Helen Wayne met Allen as he came up to the
wagon. She had some hardtack in one hand and the
canteen in the other. "Drink some of this," she said,
handing the water to him.

Allen tilted the canteen to his lips and let some of
the brackish water trickle into his mouth. He handed it
back and took the hardtack.

"Lordy, I thought Mick was going to kill you,"
Helen said.

"So did I."

"I . . . I'm glad he didn't." The words were slow,
hesitant, but when Allen looked up, he saw that her
pale blue eyes were watching him intently.

"So am I," he replied, summoning up a weak grin.
Even under these circumstances, his inbred politeness
made him go on, "Thank you for the food and water."

"Oh, you're welcome," Helen said quickly. "I just wish it was more, Mr. Kerry."

Was she blushing? Impossible, Allen thought. "This is fine," he told her. "Just fine."

Her shy smile got wider.

Lacey watched for a moment as Allen took the food and water from Helen, but then she turned to search the rude camp for Tucker McCall. She spotted him, sitting by himself on his horse, and walked over to him.

He saw her coming and waited, saying nothing as she came up beside his stirrup.

"I wanted to thank you," Lacey said. "I'm sure you saved Allen's life."

"Mick and I would have had it out sooner or later," Tucker replied. "Just so happened it came today."

"Well, I still appreciate it. And I'm sorry about the . . . the things that Allen said to you."

Tucker waved a big hand. "Don't you worry about that." He kept his eyes on the horizon now, as if he did not want to look at her.

Was he angry with her, she wondered, or was he just shy? On an impulse, she stuck her hand up to him. "I'm Lacey Ellis," she said. "And you're Tucker McCall. Helen told me your name."

Tucker hesitated and then took her hand for a second, his big paw swallowing her fingers. Her skin was cool and soft, just as he had imagined. He dropped her hand as quickly as he could.

"Glad to meet you, ma'am. Wish it was under better conditions."

Helen had said practically the same thing to her, Lacey thought. "Do you think we'll get out of this mess alive, Mr. McCall?" she asked bluntly.

"I don't rightly know, ma'am. I hope so. I'm not ready to depart from this life just yet."

Lacey smiled up at him. "Neither am I, Mr. McCall. Thank you again."

He touched the brim of his hat and nodded. "Ma'am."

Lacey walked back to the wagon. Some of the hunters were already riding out, and Burl Wayne was yelling at the others to get moving. He made no move to oppose Tucker McCall when Tucker told the men from the stage that they could use Mick's horse, giving them two mounts to share, one with a saddle. Eleanora and Rico were already on the wagon, Eleanora on the seat by herself at the moment. Rico was perched on the hides, and Lacey nimbly joined him there while Helen made a last-minute check on her team.

Allen stood beside the wagon. Lacey asked him, "Are you all right, Allen?"

"I'm fine," he said stolidly. "You just take care of yourself, Lacey. Don't worry about me."

He was still being stiff-necked, Lacey thought. His pride had been hurt, and for a man like Allen Kerry, that was just about the worst injury he could suffer.

Tucker rode up to where Helen was adjusting the harness on one of the mules. He leaned over from the saddle and reached out with a long arm to tap her on the shoulder. Helen jumped a bit, startled, then said, "Oh, it's you, Tucker."

"Best get moving," Tucker told her. "We've got a long way to go yet."

That was certainly true, Lacey thought. They were miles from any sort of safety, and the Indians could reappear at any moment.

But even in this time of danger, she found herself thinking about Tucker, about how different he was from the other buffalo hunters. He was intelligent and soft-spoken, not coarse like the others. And while there was no denying that he was a dangerous man, he was no bully, like Burl Wayne. He also was an attractive man, once you got past that rough-hewn exterior. There was a strength to him, the kind of strength that a life on the frontier bred into a man.

Once again, the caravan got under way.

Chapter Seven

Miles to the north of the fleeing group, a party of Comanche warriors drew rein and halted their horses as their chief raised his hand for them to stop. Spread out in front of the group was a pile of luggage, clothes, papers, and other personal belongings. Nearby was the abandoned hide wagon with its broken axle.

The war chief of this band, a tall, strong-featured man in his thirties named Bear Running, slipped down from his pony and walked over to the debris. He nudged one of the bags with his foot and grimaced, disturbed by this evidence of the white man's presence. The white man and his leavings had no place out here on the plains.

Hatred burned brightly at all times in Bear Running's breast, and its flame blazed up now. He wanted all the white invaders either dead or driven out of his land, nothing less. When word had reached him that Chief Quanah was chasing a group of the men who hunted the buffalo, Bear Running had gathered his braves and set out to join the pursuit. He wanted to be there to take part in the killing, and he had sent smoke signals on ahead to pass that word to Quanah.

Chief Quanah was the son of Naduah, the captive white woman. He was a mighty chief with many followers, yet he would honor the wishes of Bear Running if he could. There were upwards of fifty warriors in Bear Running's band at the moment, and he was not a man to be ignored.

Bear Running turned away from the scattered luggage and saw the eagerness on the faces of his men. With a sharp gesture, he gave them leave to do what they wanted. They swarmed forward, dismounting and poking through what the despised white men had left behind. With much laughter and whooping, they tried on the clothes, taking the most pleasure in the dresses of the women. They used their knives to cut up the bags and shred the clothes they did not take for themselves.

Bear Running held himself aloof from this frolicking. A war chief did not indulge in such games, though if he was wise he allowed his men to do so on occasion. Instead, he went over to a pile of books that had fallen from one of the cheap cases.

Picking up one of the books, Bear Running fluttered the pages and ran his fingertips over the black binding. He could not read the white man's scratchings, but he recognized the book. He had seen the mission priests with books like this one, and he knew that the white men used its teachings to justify all manner of evils against the People.

A sudden gust of wind caught at the pages and flipped them. The wind continued to blow from the north, bringing a chill with it. Bear Running looked down at the book in his hand for a moment more and then let his anger rise up and take control of him. He grabbed a handful of the fluttering pages and ripped them from the book, tossing them into the air to be carried away helter-skelter by the wind. He kept tearing out the pages and casting them away from him until the book was nothing but an empty black husk. He threw it into the dirt at his feet and spat on it.

The wind kept blowing, harder now and colder.

Bear Running turned to his men and ordered them to mount up. The time for play was over. They had to catch up to Quanah. When they did, the combined forces would move in on the foolish white men, and there would be much blood spilled. Yes, much white blood would soak into the land of the People.

Bear Running and his warriors galloped on, in front of the rising storm.

Like the day before, the temperature was hot, only today the south wind was gone. The air was still and heavy, making it a little hard to breathe as the stagecoach, the wagon, and the hunters moved on through the morning into early afternoon.

On the wagon seat, Lacey Ellis was handling the reins. Helen was tired after driving all night and morning, and Lacey had convinced her to switch places for a while. As she swayed on the seat beside Lacey, Helen said, "Sure is hot again today. It feels more like summer than spring."

"There's a saying down here in Texas," Lacey told her. "If you don't like the weather, just wait a few minutes."

Eleanora spoke up from her position just behind the seat, where she had moved at Lacey's insistence. Her voice was bitter as she said, "The weather down here is awful, just like everything else."

Lacey did not feel like arguing with her. She kept her mouth shut and concentrated on driving the team.

The hunters were spread out around the wagon and the coach, as before, with Tucker McCall and Burl Wayne riding at the front of the group. Trailing behind were the ones on foot, joined at the moment by Rico Lopez, who had insisted that he wanted to walk part of the way with his father. Antonio had not protested too much, since he obviously missed his son while Rico was riding on the wagon.

The men on foot were more spread out today, each setting his own pace. At the front, Willie was taking his turn on the mule, with Ben Proctor riding beside him on Mick's horse. Antonio and Rico seemed the strongest of the walkers, and they were able to stay the closest to the wagon. Louis Shepherd came along next, with Allen Kerry bringing up the rear.

"Lord, but I could do with a drink," Proctor said as he wiped sweat from his forehead and glanced over at Willie on the mule.

"Maybe next time we stop, that lady on the wagon will give us some more water," Willie suggested.

Proctor snorted in derision. "I ain't talkin' about water, boy. I need some whiskey."

Willie was well aware that Proctor kept a bottle in the boot under the driver's seat of the coach. He had never seen Proctor drinking while he was handling the reins, but he knew the older man drank heavily when he was not working.

Willie remembered when he hired on with the stage line as a guard. At the time he had been glad that they put him to work with an old hand like Ben Proctor. But in the eighteen months since then, he had seen how bitter and unpleasant Proctor really was, and he had started to wish he had a different partner.

It looked as if it didn't matter much now. Willie did not expect to get out of this alive. Just because the Indians were leaving them alone right now didn't mean they wouldn't be back.

Which meant that it wouldn't hurt to ask Ben Proctor the question he had always wanted to ask.

"Ben," Willie said, "how come you're such an ornery ol' coot, anyway?"

Proctor shot an angry glance at the younger man. "What the hell kind of question is that?" he demanded.

"I was just curious. You seem like you've got a grudge against the world, Ben. You've been like that ever since I met you. Reckon I just wondered why."

Proctor did not say anything for a moment as he rode alongside the mule. Then he spoke up, "You figure we're all goin' to die, so it don't matter if you hurt my feelin's, is that it, boy?"

Willie shook his head. "Didn't mean to hurt your feelings, Ben. I just wanted to know."

"My life ain't none of your damn business," Proctor growled. Then he sighed and shook his head. "Don't reckon it would hurt none to tell you, though. Just don't let any of this get around, you hear?"

Willie grinned and nodded his head. "You can count on me, Ben."

"I'd better be able to. . . . Well, to make a long

story short, I was married once. Hell, I reckon I still am. She never did divorce me. She just left."

Suddenly, Willie Morse began to wish he had not given in to his curiosity and probed into Proctor's past. A man deserved his privacy, even an old razorback like Ben Proctor. But now that the stage driver had begun talking, he seemed to want to continue.

"The woman leavin' wasn't the worst of it," he said. "A man misses a wife's touch, but he can live without it. The worst thing was that she took our young'un with her."

"You had a kid?" Willie let his surprise show in his voice and instantly regretted it.

Proctor glowered up at him. "What the hell's wrong with that? Of course I had a kid, prettiest little girl you ever did see." His voice grew softer and huskier as he went on, "I reckon the thing I missed the most was the way she used to watch for me when she knew I was comin' in from a run. Her face sure did light up when she saw me comin'." He shook his head and paused for a moment, and when he resumed, his tone of voice was bleak. "That's been over a long time ago. My wife didn't like the way I made my livin', always gone from home, pushin' the coaches along. So one time when I got back, my little girl wasn't waitin' for me. Nobody was waitin' for me." He fell silent.

Willie endured the silence for a few moments, as long as he could, and then said, "Hell, I'm sorry, Ben. I didn't mean to bring up a lot of old memories."

Proctor turned his head and spat. "It don't matter," he said harshly. "Nothin' does, not anymore."

Willie understood now, and wished that he did not. If he had been in the same situation as Ben Proctor, he might have felt the same way, might have been just as surly and unfriendly.

Louis Shepherd watched as Proctor and Willie talked, but he paid no attention to what the two stage-line employees were saying. He had his own problems, and it took most of his energy just to keep plodding along.

The heat was getting to Shepherd. He was aware of that fact, but he was too tired to do anything about it.

Anyway, there was not much he could do. He kept his hat on to shield his head from the sun, but the still, heavy air was making it hard for him to breathe.

As he walked, his mind wandered of its own accord back over his life. It was nothing to be proud of. He had been a young man when he discovered his ability to charm women, especially older women. Since then his career had consisted of one money-making scheme after another, always financed by some lonely woman whom he had seduced. It was appallingly easy for him to work his way into their favor, and it did not matter to him if they were young or old, married, single, or widowed. He gave them what they wanted, and they gave him what he needed—money. This latest masquerade of his, as a Bible salesman, was only an excuse to move around and meet a large number of women. His so-called profession, with its religious overtones, gave his liaisons an illicit air that made them that much more exciting. Nothing attracted women like the twin lures of passion and sin.

To Shepherd's surprise, however, he was beginning to realize that his relationship with Eleanora Morrison was taking on a different tone.

At first he had viewed her only as a way to get out of Texas. He had planned to wrap her around his finger so that she would take him with her when she returned to the East. Once there, he could discard her as he had all the lonely women before her. But when he saw the pain and humiliation that their current ordeal was causing her, he felt genuine sympathy for her. It was the first emotion he had felt in years, other than concern for himself. Could it be that he was actually starting to care for her?

He would never find out for sure. He was convinced that all of them would die out here on these desolate plains. That was the way his luck was running these days.

Up at the front of the group, Tucker said to Burl Wayne, "Think I'll check our back trail."

"Good idea," Wayne agreed. "See if you can hurry up the wagon and that stagecoach."

Tucker swung his horse around and headed toward the rear of the group. He did not see how Wayne expected them to move any faster as long as they were burdened with the hides, but it did not do any good to talk to the man.

As he approached the wagon he saw that Lacey Ellis was handling the reins now. That was a good idea, if she was capable of the task. Helen could use a rest every now and then. It looked like Lacey was doing a good job of driving the balky mules.

"Is everything all right, Tucker?" Helen asked as he rode up.

"For right now," he answered. "No sign of trouble. I just thought I'd check our back trail." He grinned. "By the way, Burl says to pick up the pace back here."

Lacey snorted. "Then let him come back and pull along with the mules," she said caustically. She glanced at the woman on the seat beside her and went on, "I'm sorry, Helen, but your brother's not the most pleasant man I've ever met."

"You don't have to apologize to me," Helen told her. "I know how Burl is."

"I'd best get on back," Tucker said. He nodded to the women, noticing that Eleanora was still sullen and withdrawn. Then he turned his horse again and rode off.

The men on foot were trailing a little farther behind today, Tucker saw. It was too much to expect them to keep up, not after walking all night and half the day today. Willie Morse nodded to him as he rode by, but Proctor did not look up. He waved to Antonio and Rico and got a grin from Rico in return. As Tucker approached Louis Shepherd, the man raised a hand, hailing him. Tucker drew rein to see what he wanted.

"What can I do for you, mister?" Tucker asked, leaning on his saddle horn.

"My name is Louis Shepherd, sir. I noticed yesterday that you seemed somewhat sympathetic to our plight. I was wondering if you could do anything to persuade your leader to let us dump those hides and ride in the coach."

Tucker slowly shook his head. "Wish I could, but you don't know Burl Wayne. He's not going to part with those hides unless he has to. And right now, his men are willing to back him up. They see those hides— and what they're worth—as their future."

Shepherd's face sagged in disappointment. There was something in his eyes that Tucker did not like as he said, "My God, man, are you saying that those hides are more important than human lives?"

"That's the way Burl Wayne looks at it," Tucker said bluntly.

"Someone should shoot that man," Shepherd muttered.

"Could be, but I wouldn't advise you to try it. He'd kill you without thinking twice. And he's got more than enough guns on his side to back him up."

Tucker left Shepherd talking to himself. He resolved to keep a closer eye on the Bible salesman; there could be trouble coming from that direction.

As if they needed any more trouble . . .

Allen saw Tucker coming and hoped that the big buckskin-clad scout would ride on by. Tucker reined in, though, and asked, "How are you doing back here?"

"I'm fine," Allen said. He wasn't about to tell Tucker how badly his feet hurt, or how his legs were numb with exhaustion.

Tucker did not need to be told. He could see what kind of shape Allen was in. He was marching along stubbornly, evidently intending not to complain no matter how bad things got.

"I've got a pair of winter moccasins in my bag you're welcome to. They'll be a mite hot, but better'n those shoes for walking."

Shaking his head, Allen said, "I don't need them."

"Don't reckon I'd be holding up as well as you if I had to walk like this," Tucker told him. "You're a brave man, my friend."

Allen just looked at him. "I'm sure you really feel that way."

The sarcasm in his voice made Tucker angry. "Sounds like you're calling me a liar, and that doesn't

sit well out here, Allen. You'd best remember that.
And I meant what I said about you."

He spurred away, leaving Allen to trudge on ahead.
Allen knew his comment had been uncalled for, but he
was still chagrined over the fact that Tucker had had to
save his life this morning. Maybe Tucker did feel some
honest admiration for him; if so, Allen did not want it.
The last thing he wanted was to impress Tucker McCall.

Still, he realized that there was a great deal he
could learn from Tucker—if they got out of this mess
alive. Tucker had obviously been out here in the West
for years, maybe all his life. He would know all the
tricks of staying alive on the frontier.

And some demon in Allen's mind was telling him
that he wanted to learn these things. He would show
Lacey that he was perfectly capable of surviving out
here. Then, having demonstrated his competency, he
could walk away without feeling like an utter, helpless
fool. He could return to Boston, leaving Lacey to make
her decision: She could return with him to civilization
. . . or stay out here in the wilderness with louts like
Tucker McCall.

His chin firm and his back straight, Allen Kerry
marched on, listening to his own drum.

As Tucker headed north and left the group behind,
he felt the first cool touch of a breeze on his beard-
stubbled face. He kept his horse at an even, ground-
eating trot and put a mile or so between himself and
the hunters. The breeze was very faint, sometimes
there and sometimes not, but it promised a change in
the weather, a relief from this stifling heat.

Far away on the northern horizon, he saw a low
band of clouds. There was something closer that was
more interesting, however—dust.

The last two days had dried out the ground enough
so that the horses would raise a little dust again. There
was a faint plume of it hanging in the air several miles
back, and as Tucker studied it, he felt a chill that had
nothing to do with the temperature.

Maybe the dust came from another bunch of buffalo hunters, he thought; there were plenty of them

around this year. But even as the thought crossed his mind, he knew how unlikely that was. That dust was being raised by the hooves of Indian ponies, he was sure of that.

He sat his horse for several long minutes, trying to chart the progress of the dust. It did not seem to be moving very fast, which meant that the pursuers were not making any great effort to catch up.

They're still playing with us, he thought. It was a cruel form of cat and mouse, but there was nothing he or any of the others could do about it. All they could do was keep going and hope they found someplace to fort up before the final attack came.

He glanced at the horizon again and saw that even though the trailing dust was not moving very fast, the clouds were. They were visibly closer now, and the wind out of the north felt slightly stronger.

Tucker frowned as he watched the clouds. There was nothing more changeable than spring weather in the Texas Panhandle, according to the stories he had heard even up in Kansas. He knew from experience how quickly a storm could blow up on the Kansas plains, and he figured the weather to be just as intense down here in Texas. The clouds were dark and thick; he did not like the way they looked.

He turned and sent the horse into a gallop back toward the hunters.

This time he did not stop to talk to anyone until he reached the front of the caravan. Burl Wayne was waiting for him. "Any Indian sign?" Wayne asked as soon as Tucker had reined in.

"There's some dust back there," Tucker said. "It's not moving any faster than we are, though. We've got other problems."

Wayne frowned at him. "What are you talkin' about?"

"There's a storm coming."

Wayne stared at him for a long moment, then exploded, "A storm! What the blue blazes is wrong with you, McCall? We got Comanches on our tail, and you're worried about some damn storm!"

"Looks like a bad one," Tucker insisted. "And it's moving toward us pretty fast. I think we should start looking around for some cover."

"I ain't gonna worry about some storm when we got them savages behind us," Wayne snapped. "We're puttin' as much ground behind us as we can."

Tucker felt his anger building until it could no longer be contained. "You're the stubbornest, greediest son of a bitch I've ever seen!" he growled.

Wayne's lips pulled back from his teeth in an enraged grimace. He was carrying his rifle across the pommel of his saddle, and he swung the muzzle of it toward Tucker with a snarl. "You don't like the way I do things, you can get the hell out of here and take your chances on your own!"

"Reckon I might be better off if I did. You'd probably shoot me in the back as soon as I started off, though."

Tucker saw the pure and simple hatred in Wayne's eyes as the little man replied, "Someday you and me are gonna have this out, McCall."

"Someday," Tucker grunted. He jerked his horse's head around and headed for the wagon, unwilling to continue this argument.

Maybe he should just ride out, he thought. It was not the first time he had considered the idea—but he could not bring himself to abandon the stage passengers. He and Helen were the only ones who cared about them.

He could not leave Lacey here to die. The thought burst through his mind with power and clarity. *I can't leave Lacey.*

He was not sure he knew what he felt for her; all he knew was that whatever trouble came, he wanted to be there to face it with her.

As he pulled up next to the wagon, Lacey said, "There's a storm coming, isn't there?"

"How'd you know?"

"I've spent a lot of time in Texas, remember? I know how still it was earlier, and I felt that wind start

coming out of the north. I'd say we're in for a good
spring thunderstorm."

"We've had some bad storms up in Kansas," Helen
put in. "What are they like down here?"

"Humdingers," Lacey said. "I remember a few
years back when a cyclone came through my father's
ranch. It tore up the bunkhouse and knocked down
trees, not to mention all the cattle that it killed. Luckily
it missed the main house."

Eleanora had been listening to Lacey, and now she
turned her head and looked behind them. The clouds
were closer and still advancing, and the wind whipped
at the shawl wrapped around her shoulders. The look
on her face was one of resigned despair, as if she had
come to expect nothing but more trouble.

Lacey went on, "Rico's back there walking with his
father. Will you go get him, Tucker? I'd like to have
him here on the wagon with us if there's going to be a
storm."

"Good idea," Tucker said, nodding. "I'll tend to
it."

As he spurred away, Lacey turned to Helen and
said, "Tucker certainly is different from those other
hunters. He really seems to care about people."

"Yes, he does," Helen replied, a slightly wistful
tone in her voice. She had seen the way Tucker was
looking at Lacey, and she knew what was happening here
—even if Tucker and Lacey did not yet. She also knew
there was not one damn thing she could do about it.

Antonio and Rico looked up at Tucker as he reined
in and slipped down out of the saddle. Holding the
reins of his horse, Tucker said, "How about riding back
up to the wagon with me, Rico?"

Rico shook his head. "I am not tired, Señor Tucker.
I will walk with my father."

Tucker knelt beside the boy. "I'm not sure that
would be a good idea, son."

Antonio heard the urgency in Tucker's voice and
said, "Is there going to be more trouble, señor?"

"Looks like there's a storm coming. We think it
might be a pretty bad one."

"Rico, I want you to go back to the wagon," Antonio said firmly.

"But Papa, I want to be with you."

"I know. But it may be safer for you with Señorita Lacey. You remember some of the bad storms at the ranch?"

Rico nodded.

"You go with Señor McCall now," Antonio said softly. "Do not worry. We will be together again."

Tucker scooped up the boy and climbed into the saddle with him. Though he was not happy about leaving his father, Rico was excited to be on the back of Tucker's tall horse. Tucker nodded to Antonio and said, "Keep an eye on those clouds."

"*Sí*, I will."

Tucker gauged the movement of the approaching storm and decided he had the time to warn the others. He rode over to Proctor and Willie, who had already noticed the dark clouds. "When it hits, we'll hunt a hole," Proctor told him.

Shepherd gave no response but a weary nod when Tucker spoke to him. But Allen Kerry frowned, looked back at the clouds, and said, "Will you keep an eye on Lacey and my sister, McCall?"

"I have been," Tucker replied. "The wagon should give them some shelter."

He turned the horse and kneed it into a gallop, which brought an excited laugh from Rico. As they rode, Tucker thought about what Allen had said. The Easterner's first and only concern was for Lacey and Eleanora. The prospect of being caught out here on foot in a storm did not seem to worry him.

It was hard to figure out a man like Allen Kerry. Sometimes he came across as an insensitive bastard, while at others he could say and do the most admirable things. Which made him about like most people, Tucker supposed, even if he did come from Boston.

Tucker pulled up beside the wagon and swung Rico over onto the hides, lifting the boy effortlessly. "There you go," Tucker said. "You mind Miss Lacey and Miss Helen, understand?"

"Sí," Rico replied. "Thank you for the ride, Señor Tucker."

Tucker nodded and then grabbed for his hat as a sudden gust of wind threatened to lift it from his head. He looked back and saw the sunlight disappearing as the clouds moved in. There was a line of darkness advancing like a freight train across the plains. Tucker saw the men on foot break into a trot, which had to be agonizing for their sore feet. Their hunched shoulders told him that the rain had arrived where they were.

He turned his head and barked at Lacey, "Get that wagon moving. Now!"

Lacey whipped up the mules, and the wagon picked up speed, as did the stagecoach up ahead. The driver of the coach was looking over his shoulder apprehensively.

Tucker glanced back to check the storm, and suddenly the rain hit. There was nothing gradual about this downpour. It was a cold, wet, hard slap in the face. Tucker gasped, blinking and shaking his head to get the water out of his eyes. His horse shied wildly, trying to escape from the driving rain. But there was no place to hide.

The rain fell in blinding sheets, pounding at the caravan. Though it was early in the afternoon, the sky was almost as dark as night. The only time anyone could see was when lightning flashed, followed by the roar and rumble of thunder.

"Hold up there!" Tucker shouted at the top of his lungs, trying to be heard over the shriek of the wind. They could not go on, not in this. There was no way to tell where they were going. But neither was there shelter out here in the plains. They would just have to wait out the storm as best they could. The next moment he heard some of the other men yelling for the rest of the group to stop.

In the glare of a lightning strike, Tucker saw the wagon. He slipped down out of the saddle and then hauled hard on the reins, trying to bring the terrified horse back under control. He pulled the horse over to the wagon, using the great strength in his arms and shoulders. Lacey was trying to hold the mules and was having a hard time of it. Helen had a grip on the reins as well, and both women were working hard to keep the team from bolting. Tucker tied his horse to the back of the wagon and then sprang to the seat, pushing between Lacey and Helen. He grabbed the reins from the women and held on tightly. Slowly, feeling his firm grip on the lines, the team began to calm down, and after several minutes, they stood still, heads down, letting the rain pour over them.

Tucker glanced at Lacey and then at Helen. Both women were soaked, their clothes plastered wetly to their bodies, their hair hanging in dripping strands. Tucker looked back at the bed of the wagon and saw that Eleanora and Rico had burrowed down into the hides, pulling some of the reeking pelts over them to shield them from the rain.

Tucker gave the reins to Helen and shouted, "Hang on!" He vaulted off the seat. "I don't like the way that wind sounds! You stay here for now! I'm going to look for some shelter!"

It was doubtful he would find much in the way of shelter, but he felt he had to try. With his shoulders hunched against the force of the wind, he set out from the wagon on foot.

With visibility so poor, Tucker felt cut off from the rest of the group. He could hear men shouting and horses whinnying in fear, but he could not see them until they were right on him. More than once, he had to dodge riders who came bolting out of the torrent.

Even if by some miracle he were to locate shelter, would he be able to find his way back to the wagon?

Tucker stumbled and fell. He caught himself on his hands, his fingers sinking into the mud. He was on a slope, and he waited there for the next flash of lightning. When it came, he saw that he had stumbled into a shallow gully about five feet wide, cut into the plains by some forgotten stream. It was three feet deep, no more.

The wind was blowing even harder now, its wail deafening.

Tucker pushed himself to his feet and turned in

what he hoped was the direction of the wagon. Lacey's story about the cyclone that had struck her father's ranch was prominent in his mind. This was just the type of storm that could breed a tornado. The little gully was better than no protection at all.

He was walking into the wind now, bending almost double to make any headway. Every few feet he raised his head and called, "Lacey! Helen!" With the wind in his face he did not really expect them to hear him, but if they did, they could shout back, making it easier for him to find them.

He had gone what seemed like a mile when he suddenly heard his name being called. It was faint but definitely there. He altered his course slightly, plunged on ahead, and several minutes later saw the wagon's bulk looming up in front of him.

To Tucker's surprise, Allen Kerry was there, holding on to the side of the wagon. He must have caught up while the wagon was stopped, though his finding it in this storm was strictly luck. Tucker leaned against the other side of the wagon and told them, "There's a gully over there! Come on!"

"A gully's no shelter!" Allen shouted in reply.

"It is from a tornado!"

Lacey turned a rain-slicked face toward Allen and said, "Tucker's right, Allen! Come on!" She jumped down from the seat of the wagon, slipped in the mud as she landed, and suddenly found herself being supported by Tucker, who had reached out to grasp her arm as she fell.

Tucker waited until she had her feet back under her, then released her and reached into the wagon for Rico. As he lifted the boy out of the vehicle, Rico cried, "Papa! Where is Papa?"

Tucker had no idea where Antonio Lopez was, but he told Rico, "We'll find him! Right now you come with us!"

It took urging from both Lacey and Allen to convince Eleanora to leave the wagon, but leave it she did when it started rocking in the wind. With Tucker in the lead, the little group set out.

From somewhere—it was impossible to tell where in this maelstrom—came a rumbling sound that quickly grew in volume. Tucker remembered the sound of the trains he had ridden as a young man, and this rumble sounded a lot like that. He knew what it was.

"Come on!" he yelled to the others as he broke into an awkward run. The gully was up ahead somewhere, and they had to reach it quickly.

The others ran after him, the group stringing out somewhat. Tucker looked for the gully every time the lightning flashed, but he did not see it until he almost fell into it. "Down here!" he cried, not knowing if the others could hear him. The roar of the approaching cyclone was so loud that it seemed to be shaking the whole state of Texas.

Tucker saw Lacey stumbling toward him. He reached out for her, wrapping his arms around her and throwing both of them full length into the gully. Allen Kerry, hurrying along next to Helen Wayne, saw what Tucker had done and knew that he had better do the same. He grabbed Helen and flung her forward into the depression, diving after her and shielding her body with his own.

That left Rico and Eleanora exposed to the full fury of the storm. As they ran along side by side, the boy tugged at her skirt, shouting, "Come on, señora, come on!" Eleanora was sobbing with fear and exhaustion, but Rico would not let her slow down.

They reached the edge of the gully and went sprawling into its meager shelter.

If the roaring of the wind had been loud before, it was nothing to what came next.

The six forms huddled on the bottom of the gully as the whirling black mouth of the tornado spun along the ground toward them, ripping up small bushes and even the newly formed blades of grass. Then the funnel seemed to skip, lifting slightly as it passed over the gully.

Tucker saw sparks dancing in the air and felt what seemed like giant hands try to pluck him up into the air. Lacey had her face against his shoulder, her mouth

only inches from his ear, and still he could barely hear
her scream. Muddy water splashed in his face, and it
took him a moment to realize that the floor of the gully
had now become a stream, the runoff from the rain
sluicing through it. The water was swift but shallow.
Tucker lifted his head from it and helped Lacey hold
hers up so that she could breathe.

Then the cyclone was past, and the roaring stopped
as suddenly as it had begun.

Tucker pushed himself up onto hands and knees
and looked around. Lacey was all right, he was fairly
sure. A few feet away, Allen and Helen were in much
the same shape, covered with mud but conscious and
looking around. A little further along, Eleanora lay still
and silent. Close beside her was Rico Lopez. Rico was
stirring, and when he saw that Eleanora was not, he
reached over to her and began to shake her. "Señora!"
he called urgently. "Señora!"

Eleanora turned her head to the side, out of the
water, and drew a deep gasping breath. A sob wracked
her sodden body. "When will it stop?" she wailed. "Oh,
my God, when?"

The rain, it appeared, was abating now. Like most
spring thunderstorms, this one was small but intense. It
moved on quickly, leaving behind a welter of mud and
a stretch of ground torn up by the tornado, looking as if
it had been plowed.

The rain falling now was gentle as it washed some
of the mud off Lacey's face. She looked up at Tucker
and said softly, "You saved our lives."

He knuckled grit out of his eyes. "Hell, I was just
trying to save my own skin. You just got in my way."

"Sure." Lacey grinned at him.

Allen helped Helen to her feet and asked, "Are
you all right?" When she nodded weakly, he turned to
Eleanora and did the same. Eleanora was crying, and
Allen folded her into his arms, patting her on the back
and trying to comfort her.

Tucker stepped up out of the gully and looked
around at the bedraggled group. There were men lying
on the ground in several places, but they were slowly

getting to their feet and seemed to be all right except for looking like wet rats. The wagon was intact, the mules standing as they had been left. The stagecoach, however, was on its side, the load of hides from the top spilled out on the ground. The coach appeared to have been toppled by the winds but not hit directly by the tornado—for if it had, it would have been kindling by now. The team had been pulled over by their harness, and from the way some of the six horses were screaming and kicking, Tucker figured they were injured.

Most of the unharnessed horses were running loose. Burl Wayne had caught one and was galloping around in a frenzy, trying to pull the others back together. He yelled for some of the men to help round them up and then gestured for the rest to gather around the stagecoach. "Get it back upright!" he shouted. "Come on, we've got to get it back on its wheels!" When the men were slow to react, Wayne howled, "I'll kill the next man who don't jump!"

They knew he meant it and went to work. First the men unhitched the horses, being careful to avoid the flailing hooves. Four of them were uninjured, but the other two had broken legs and had to be shot. Next the men put their hands against the top of the coach and braced themselves to push. The coach was heavy, but with much grunting and groaning, the hunters got it upright again.

It took longer to round up the saddle horses, as well as the mule that had thrown Willie Morse. The second mule still had a limp. After satisfying himself that the mule's limp was much better, Burl Wayne announced that the mules would be added to the stage team to replace the lost horses. A couple of the saddle horses could not be found, and so Wayne gave one of his men Mick's horse and told the other to ride on the stagecoach with Duffy. The men from the stagecoach would have to make do on foot.

None of the hunters had been killed in the storm, though several had cuts and bruises from flying debris. Ben Proctor, Willie Morse, and Louis Shepherd were all unhurt, though they were wet and miserable like everyone else. The best moment in the cleanup effort came when Antonio and Rico were reunited. Both father and son were all right, and when Antonio heard from Tucker how Rico had helped save Eleanora, he beamed with pride.

Tucker and Lacey stood beside the wagon as the hides were loaded back onto the coach under Wayne's watchful eye. "I suppose we were lucky," Lacey said. "Nobody was hurt very badly, and the Indians haven't bothered us."

"I imagine the Indians had as much trouble with the storm as we did," Tucker said. "If nothing else, it ought to slow them down for a while. If we had really been lucky, that cyclone would have hit the wagon and the coach."

"Lucky, you say?"

"That way the hides would have been carried off to kingdom come," Tucker explained. "Wayne wouldn't have any reason to slow things down then. We could cut and run."

"There wouldn't be enough horses for all of us, though."

"We could double up and make better time than we have with the wagon and the coach," Tucker said bitterly.

Lacey put her hand on his arm. "We've made it this far," she said. "Maybe we'll make it a little farther."

"Let's go!" Wayne called. "Movin' out! Movin' out!"

Soaked, mud drenched, miserable—but alive—the party started on its way again.

Chapter Eight

By the time an hour had passed, it was hard to tell that there had ever been a storm. The sun was shining brightly, drying the clothes of the hunters and passengers and warming away their chill. Wayne had been pushing them hard ever since they pulled out. It was likely that the Indians had had to go to ground during the storm, just like the fleeing hunters, but they couldn't count on that slowing down the pursuit for very long.

The effects of the headlong flight were beginning to be felt. When one of the hunters suddenly stopped his horse, dismounted, and leaned exhaustedly against the animal, Wayne yelled at him to get moving again. The man ignored him. Wayne's face purpled in rage, but as he reached for his gun to threaten the man, several other hunters stopped and started to get off their horses, paying no attention to Wayne's shouting and cursing. They had been willing to follow Wayne . . . but only so far.

The ordeal was taking its toll, and if Burl Wayne did not permit the men to rest, he risked having a full-scale revolt on his hands. He could bully and threaten all he wanted, but he could not shoot all of the men, and they knew it.

Seething, he left his gun in its holster and called, "All right, we'll rest for five minutes."

Helen, again at the reins of the wagon, hauled the mules to a stop, set the brake, and stepped down from the box. Lacey joined her on the ground, but Eleanora

stayed where she was. Rico was walking with his father;
he had refused to be parted from Antonio again.

The group on foot was not far behind the wagon,
and they caught up quickly once the hunters stopped.
Helen gave them water from the barrel on the wagon.
Lacey was talking to Allen when Tucker McCall rode
up.

"Reckon I could talk to you for a few minutes,
ma'am?" Tucker asked.

"Of course, Mr. McCall," she replied. "What is
it?"

"You probably know this country better than any of
the rest of us," Tucker said, hooking a leg around the
pommel of his saddle. "Have you seen any landmarks
that might tell you where we are?"

Lacey gestured at the surrounding plains. "One
thing this part of the country is short on is landmarks. I
know we're somewhere north of the Canadian River
because we haven't crossed it yet."

Ben Proctor slouched up from the back of the
wagon to join the conversation. "We're east of the
regular stage route, I know," he put in. "What have
you got in mind, McCall?"

"I was thinking that we might need a place to fort
up," Tucker said. "I just don't think we'll make it all the
way to Adobe Walls without the Indians jumping us
again. At least we've got plenty of ammunition for both
the buffalo rifles and the Winchesters."

Proctor rubbed his jaw and considered. "The stage
line used to run through here," he said after a moment's thought. "The way was a little easier farther
west, though, so they moved it. There might be some
deserted way stations over here in this neck of the
woods. Probably ruins by now."

"That's better than nothing," Tucker said. "I think
I might do some scouting around." He touched the
brim of his hat, nodded to Lacey, and rode back toward
the front of the group.

Lacey watched him ride away and then turned to
speak to Allen. He was not there, however. He was
several yards away, talking to Helen Wayne.

Helen had caught Allen's eye while Lacey was busy, and he had walked over to her, sensing that she had something to say. He asked, "How are you feeling? That was a pretty rough storm back there."

"I'm fine," she said. "The storm is what I wanted to talk to you about, Allen."

Though she used his first name, her eyes were downcast. She seemed to be studying the toes of her boots.

After a moment, she went on, "I wanted to thank you. You saved my life when you jumped in that gully with me."

"I was just looking for a place to hide," Allen assured her. "I'm no hero."

"A hero's just a man," Helen said. "A good man. How are you getting on, Allen?" She seemed to relish the sound of his name.

"I'll be glad when we get back to civilization." He smiled. "This frontier life can be hard on the feet."

She finally looked up at him, sympathy in her blue eyes. "I'm sorry about what my brother's done to you. He had no right—"

"He had the right of a man with a gun who knows what he wants," Allen said. "Out here that seems to be all that matters."

"It's not always like that in the West. You have to be strong, all right, but not everybody is like . . . like Burl. Look at Tucker McCall," she said, nodding at the big man in buckskins.

Allen glanced over to where Tucker was talking to Lacey and Ben Proctor.

"McCall seems to be a good man," Allen said slowly.

"He is. I haven't known him long, but I've lived with my brother and men like him all my life. It doesn't take long to see that Tucker is different."

"There aren't many like him in Boston, that's certain."

A smile lit Helen's face. "Boston! I'd love to go there sometime. What's it like?"

"It's the best place to live in America," he told her. "The city is called the Cradle of Liberty because the roots of the American Revolution are there. There are a great many historical sites and museums, theaters, and an opera house, things like that."

"Have you been to all of them?"

Allen shook his head and smiled slightly. "Well, no. I tend to spend most of my time in the financial district or at my family's house on Beacon Hill."

"Is it a big house?"

"Large, perhaps, but not huge." His voice grew reminiscent. "It's a red brick town house near Louisburg Square."

"That sounds wonderful," Helen said. "I'd love to see Boston, to learn all about it. You don't learn a whole lot out here in the buffalo camps."

"You should go to school," Allen said. "Although I don't know where you could do that around here."

Helen shook her head. "There aren't many schools in this part of the country yet. And I'd feel . . . well, I'd feel funny going to school with a bunch of youngsters."

"Back east you wouldn't have to. You could hire a tutor to teach you, to get you ready to go on to a university—" Allen broke off, suddenly aware just how unlikely the things he was saying really were.

"That's a nice dream," Helen said, "but it won't come true, will it?"

Allen tried to sound reassuring as he said, "I don't know, we might get out of this mess yet. We've managed to stay alive this long."

"Even if we do get away from the Indians, I'll have to go on living like I have been. There's no place for me but with the hunters."

Allen reached out without thinking and put his hand on her arm. "I could help you," he said. Then he realized what he was doing and saying and blinked in surprise.

But the most surprising thing was that he knew he meant it. Helen Wayne deserved a chance. Just because she came from a bad background did not mean that she was worthless.

"You're just saying that."

With a firm resolve, Allen said, "No, I'm not. I

mean it, Helen. If we live through this, I'll see to it that you have your chance to go back east and get an education."

She gave him a long, thoughtful look. "Why would you do a thing like that?"

Allen cast about in his mind, trying to figure out for himself just what he was feeling. Finally, he gave up and simply said, "Because I want to."

Helen nodded slowly. "I . . . I'll think about it." She smiled at him and then moved away, turning to tend to her team.

"She'll think about what?" Lacey said from beside Allen, startling him.

"Oh! I just . . . I simply offered to help the woman go back east if she wants to, Lacey. Provided we get out of this horrible situation we're in now." Allen was a bit flustered, his face tinged with embarrassment.

"That's fine of you," Lacey told him.

"What do you mean by that?" Allen asked defensively.

"Just what I said. Helen is a good woman who has led a rough life. She deserves a chance for some happiness."

That was exactly what Allen had been thinking. He said, "That's all there was to it, I assure you."

Lacey gave him a strange look. "You don't have to explain yourself to me, Allen."

"I wasn't trying to—" he began.

"Well, you don't have to." With that, she went to speak to Antonio and Rico. Allen watched her, his head spinning with confusing thoughts that almost succeeded in making him forget how badly his feet hurt and how much his muscles ached. Almost.

Lacey's message seemed to be plain enough. She was not concerned about his interest in Helen Wayne because she no longer considered herself to have a claim on his affections. She had not come out and said that she no longer intended to marry him, but he was certain that was what she meant.

Was it because of Tucker McCall? Or had she simply realized that the two of them were not meant for each other?

And just what was his interest in Helen Wayne? Was it possible he was beginning to have romantic feelings for a woman who was little better than a prostitute? A soiled dove, as the newspapers so tactfully referred to them?

Helen Wayne was a decent woman inside, a woman who had been forced by circumstances into an unpleasant life. Allen was sure of that, though he could cite no evidence other than his instincts. He was an astute businessman, though, and as such prided himself on being a shrewd judge of character.

Abruptly, he shook his head. All this was idle speculation. There was little chance any of them would survive the next Indian attack. And another attack would come; he was sure of that.

Nearby, Burl Wayne was impatiently walking his horse back and forth when Tucker rode up to him. He should have been resting the animal, but his desire to be under way again was overruling his common sense.

"Think I'll do some scouting," Tucker said without preamble.

Wayne squinted at him. "You mean you're cuttin' and runnin' like a yellow dog," he said.

Tucker's gaze was icy as he replied, "I'm going to look for someplace we can make a stand if we have to. That stage driver says there's some old abandoned way stations around here. I thought I'd see if there's one the same direction we're going."

"Might be a good idea," Wayne admitted with a shrug. "I'm warnin' you, though, McCall—you better come back. No man runs out on me."

"I'll be back," Tucker promised flatly. "Before night."

"See that you are."

Tucker fought his anger and turned his horse around. He rode alongside the group, looking for Lacey. When he spotted her with the Lopezes, he rode over and said, "Reckon I'll do some scouting around. I'll be back before nightfall, though."

Lacey nodded. "All right." She did not ask why he had sought her out to tell her that he was leaving, and he did not volunteer anything else. He just nodded and rode away, glancing over his shoulder and returning Rico's wave.

Lacey watched his figure recede into the distance, a big man on a tall horse, and she thought, *You'd better come back, Tucker McCall. . . .*

A moment later, Burl Wayne was yelling for everyone to mount up, and this time the men went along with his command. They had rested for a few minutes, and now they were remembering that several hundred hostiles were behind them. They were as ready to move on as they were going to be.

Tucker left the group behind, but he found that his thoughts remained with them. The terrible storm had done more than soak their clothes and injure some of their horses. It had also forced him to be honest with himself about the way he felt for Lacey. Two days was not long, but sometimes it was long enough, he supposed, to know what was inside of a person.

There was nothing romantic about hiding in a gully to get away from a tornado, but Tucker remembered vividly how Lacey's slender body had felt when he had her wrapped in his arms. Maybe not knowing if any of them were going to live through the storm had intensified the experience for him.

He knew that when you got right down to it, he had been more scared for Lacey than for himself. Maybe that was part of love, too.

He wished he had said more to her before he pulled out on this scouting mission, but the words had not come. He had looked into her eyes when he had said good-bye, and he hoped that what she had seen there would help her to know how he felt.

Tucker knew that Lacey was Allen Kerry's woman. He had not done anything improper, and it would stay that way. It had been a long time since anyone had accused him of being a gentleman, but there were some rules a man did not break, no matter how much they hurt.

He kept his horse moving at a ground-eating lope, and as he rode, his eyes constantly scanned the plains.

Out here by himself like this, he would make a tempting target for even a small group of Comanches.

About an hour after leaving the others, he spotted a small plume of smoke up ahead. Tucker frowned. In this part of the country, smoke like that usually meant something bad. He spurred his horse into a gallop and then slipped his Winchester out of its boot.

There was trouble up ahead. He could feel it in his gut.

Before long he was close enough to see that whatever was burning was not very big. It was not large enough to be a building. As he drew nearer, Tucker saw that it was a wagon. He could also see several dark shapes on the ground nearby.

He pulled up, reining in and searching the surrounding area. There were no Indians in sight, but they had definitely been here. It was possible they were hiding somewhere, waiting for him to come closer. But he had to risk that; he had to see if there was anything he could do for the poor souls who had belonged with the wagon.

The Comanches had not been gone long, he saw as he directed his horse to the scene of the massacre. The blaze was still burning strongly, though it was starting to die down a bit. Holding the Winchester ready, Tucker slipped down from the saddle and knelt by one of the bodies.

It was the corpse of a good-sized man, though it was hard to tell much more than that. The Indians had done quite a job with their knives. Tucker felt his stomach lurch. They had stripped the man, staked him out, and then had their fun with him. Tucker shook his head and went over to one of the other victims.

This one, also a man, was in the same gruesome condition. A third man was nearby, but he had not been tortured. Instead, his body was riddled with arrows. Obviously, he had been killed defending the wagon, and the Comanches had preferred mutilating the captives they had taken alive.

Tucker wondered what these three men had been doing out here alone. More than likely they had been buffalo hunters, but there was no way to be sure since no weapons could be seen. The presence of a Sharps Big Fifty rifle would have confirmed it. The Indians had probably taken their weapons, as well as run off the horses.

Tucker glanced back the way he had come. The caravan was coming in this direction, and he did not want the women to see what had happened here. He could not take the time to bury the men. Instead, he swung up into the saddle and galloped back over his own trail.

It took him only a half hour to return to the group. Burl Wayne saw him coming and spurred out ahead to meet him. "Well?" Wayne demanded. "Did you find that way station?"

Tucker shook his head. "I came back because of something else I found. There's three dead men and their burned-out wagon up yonder a ways. I reckon they were buffalo hunters, too."

Wayne frowned at him. "What good does it do us to know about that, McCall? I thought you was lookin' for a place we could put up a fight."

"I think we should swing a little more west," Tucker told him. "I don't want the women to see what I saw."

Wayne stared in disbelief. "You want us to change direction because some woman might get sick to her stomach? What if we miss Adobe Walls?"

"We don't know that we're headed for it now," Tucker pointed out. "We've been angling west. I just want to go a little more in that direction. And anyway, those bodies won't help the mood of the rest of the men."

"We ain't got the time to argue about it." Wayne turned in his saddle and waved for the group to move a little more to the southwest.

When Tucker rode back to the wagon, Lacey asked, "Did you find one of the old way stations?"

Tucker shook his head. "Didn't run across one."

"Then why did we change direction?" Helen asked.

After a moment's hesitation, Tucker said, "There's been some trouble up ahead. The Indians caught a

wagon with three men in it. I figured we'd be better off
going around it."

"I can imagine why," Lacey said grimly. She glanced
up at Tucker and saw that he was looking intently to the
north. "What is it?"

Tucker lifted an arm and pointed behind them.
"We've got company again," he said.

Lacey and Helen both turned to look. At first
neither of them could see anything, but after a minute
they discerned movement on the horizon. "Indians?"
Helen asked.

Tucker nodded. "Reckon so," he said flatly. "The
ground's still wet enough from that storm blowing
through that they wouldn't raise any dust. We might've
had a little more warning if they had." He smiled and
shook his head, but there was no humor in his eyes.
"They're coming fast."

Helen sat poised on the box, ready to whip the
mules into a run. "Do we make a run for it?" she asked.

"That's all we can do." Tucker raised his voice and
shouted, "Indians behind us! Let's go! Everybody *move!*"

The other hunters took up the cry, and it was only
a matter of seconds until everyone in the party knew
that their period of grace was over.

Tucker jerked his horse around, facing toward the
Indians. Lacey called out to him. "Where are you going?"

"Somebody's got to help those men on foot," he
shot back and, spurring his horse into a gallop, took off
with a wild yell.

Helen popped the whip and slapped the reins, and
the mules broke into a run. Lacey grabbed hold of the
seat and heard Eleanora let out a dismayed moan behind her.

A minute later Burl Wayne raced past the wagon,
heading for the rear. The word had reached him that
the Indians were closing in again, and he wanted to see
the situation for himself, maybe take a few potshots at
them.

The way Burl Wayne saw it, he had a score to
settle with those painted heathens. If they had left him
alone, this hunting trip might have made him a rich man.

Tucker rode hard. He saw the men on foot running and knew that they were aware of the threat. He veered toward Antonio and Rico Lopez.

"Give me the boy and you swing up behind!" he called to Antonio as he reined in. The horse was stopped for a bare moment as Antonio handed Rico up and then climbed on behind the saddle.

"Your horse, she cannot carry all three of us!" Antonio protested as Tucker spurred the animal into motion again.

"I'm taking you to the wagon," Tucker told him. He had an arm wrapped around Rico, holding tightly to him.

The horse was a good one, full of heart, and it gave its all to the run despite the triple burden. As Tucker cut the distance between them and the wagon, Lacey spotted them coming and crawled over the back of the box into the bed of the wagon. Perched on the hides, she held out her arms as they approached. "Hand the boy to me!" she called.

Tucker drew his horse close beside the wagon, the animal racing at a dead run. "Get ready, boy!" he told Rico, then swung him toward the wagon.

Rico reached out to Lacey. Her hands caught his, and she pulled, grasping at him. Both of them fell over onto the pile of buffalo skins.

At the same time, Antonio left the back of Tucker's horse with a leap, but the jump was poorly timed, and he hit the edge of the wagon. Just as he started to slip backward, Lacey and Rico regained their balance and lunged across the bed to grab his arms, steadying him until he could pull himself all the way onto the wagon.

As soon as she saw that Antonio and Rico were safely on the wagon, Lacey turned to the big man racing his horse alongside. "Tucker!" she cried out. "You've got to help Allen!"

Tucker, already swinging his mount into a wide turn, did not waste any breath on a reply. He waved a callused hand at Lacey and then leaned forward over the neck of the galloping horse.

The Indians were still a good way off, perhaps a

half mile. As he rode toward the rear of the group,
Tucker saw that several of the hunters were falling back
to form a rear guard, among them Burl Wayne. That
surprised Tucker for a moment, until he realized that
for Wayne, fighting the Comanches amounted to protecting his investment and his profit. Wayne and the
other men dropped down off their horses, unstrapping
their heavy Sharps rifles and using the saddles as sup-
ports. The buffalo guns began to boom.

Allen Kerry was running toward Tucker but did
not seem to see him until Tucker was nearly on him.
Tucker yanked the horse to a stop and dropped out of
the saddle. "Get on!" he told Allen. Even as he spoke,
he was pulling his own Sharps loose from its straps.

Allen hesitated, unsure of what to do.

Tucker snapped, "Mount up, dammit!"

Then Allen did what he was told, scrambling up
into the saddle.

It took a strong man to fire a Big Fifty from a
standing position, but that was what Tucker McCall was
about to do. He slid a cartridge into the breech and
slapped it shut, then lifted the butt to his shoulder. He
glanced back at Allen and told him, "Get back to the
wagon!"

"Without you?" Allen asked. He was having some
trouble holding the horse. The animal danced around in
fear and confusion.

"I'm needed here," Tucker said, his words nearly
drowned out by the thunder of blasting rifles. He looked
at the Indians, took a deep breath, steadied the muzzle,
and squeezed the trigger.

The Sharps kicked back against his shoulder, jar-
ring him. He held the gun firmly enough to stop the
muzzle from climbing, though, and he knew his shot
had at least gone in the right direction. At this range it
was impossible to be sure if he had hit anything.

Sensing movement behind him, Tucker looked back
and saw that Allen was still there, still trying to hold
the horse under control. "What the hell are you waiting
for?"

"I'm not going back without you," Allen told him.

"Look, fellow, Lacey needs you—"

"How do you think she would feel about me if I left you here to die while I saved myself?" Allen demanded. "Besides, she needs you more than she needs me now, and we both know it, McCall! The woman's in love with you, dammit!"

There. It was said. And Allen Kerry, for one, was glad.

Tucker stared at him for a moment and then turned to face the oncoming Comanches. Without conscious thought, he reloaded the Sharps. Lifting it, he sighted and fired again, welcoming the deafening explosion of black powder, the hard recoil that rocked his body. He understood those things. Finally he looked back and said, "All right. Let's go."

Tucker grasped Allen's outstretched hand and let Allen help him onto the bare back of the horse. "Let's get the hell out of here," he told the Easterner.

Allen kicked the horse into a run, and Tucker hung on, holding the Sharps close to his body so as not to unbalance them. Allen bounced awkwardly in the saddle, but he stayed aboard the horse and kept it going in the right direction.

The other hunters were retreating now as well, and with them were Ben Proctor, Willie Morse, and Louis Shepherd, each riding double with one of the hunters. The hunters were hard men, but they were not going to stand by and watch while the Indians overran men on foot.

Tucker's horse, though exhausted, still had enough speed left to catch up to the wagon one more time. As they drew up alongside it, Tucker called to Allen over the pounding of hooves, "Jump for it!"

Allen glanced back at him, eyes wide. "I can't!"

"Do it!"

Allen took a deep breath, let go of the reins, kicked his feet loose from the stirrups, and leaped out of the saddle. Antonio Lopez was ready on the wagon to reach out and grab him. Both men sprawled on the hides.

Tucker shifted forward into the saddle. There had not been time to explain to Allen that he had to ride

ahead of the wagon and the stagecoach. If they were to
survive this attack, they had to find someplace to take
cover. Headlong flight would not save their lives in the
long run.

He urged the horse on to greater speed. The animal was running its heart out, and Tucker was not sure
how much longer it would last.

A little longer, he prayed. *A little longer.*

There was something up ahead on the horizon,
a darker patch on the land, and it seemed to be growing in size as they got closer. A clump of scrubby oak
trees . . .

Tucker felt his hopes leap. It was not much, but it
was better than being caught in the open. It would
have to do. He waved the group on, yelling, "Come on!
Make for the trees!"

The Indians had somewhat closed the gap, and
there was more shooting now. Helen Wayne was alone
on the box, cursing and yelling and snapping the whip.
Lacey, Allen, Eleanora, Antonio, and Rico were riding
on the hides, trying to keep from being bounced off as
the wagon rattled along. Helen saw Tucker ride into
the lead, saw him wave toward the trees. She was
already turning the wagon slightly to cut down the
distance to the clump of oak.

Tucker reached the vegetation first and saw the
reason for its existence—a small spring in a little wash,
surrounded by the oaks. There was room for the wagon
and the coach amid the trees. Tucker dropped from the
saddle and let the horse go, knowing the animal was too
tired to run off when there was water and grass here.
With the Sharps in one hand, he yanked the Winchester from its boot and then went down on one knee,
laying the rifle on the ground beside him. He reloaded
the Sharps as the other hunters began galloping up.
There would be time for one shot with the Big Fifty,
then he would start using the Winchester.

He fired the heavy rifle, flame and smoke belching
from the muzzle, and then snatched up the carbine and
began snapping shots at the charging Indians. He levered, fired, levered, fired.

The blast of gunfire all around him was like the end of the world.

Through the haze of smoke clouding the scene, he saw the wagon careening toward the trees, Helen whipping the mules like a demon. The stagecoach was slightly ahead of the wagon, and both vehicles were less than a hundred yards from the trees.

But the Indians had narrowed the gap. It was going to be close.

Tucker picked his targets and tried to aim, though he fired as rapidly as he could. Several of the Indians threw up their hands and fell from their horses, but in the cacophony of battle, it was impossible to tell whose shots had felled them.

Most of the hunters had reached the trees by now and were firing at the Indians. Ben Proctor, Willie Morse, and Louis Shepherd joined in, blazing away with rifles they had borrowed from hunters who were using buffalo guns.

On the racing wagon, the passengers were huddled down as far as they could get in the hides. The air around them was screaming with bullets. Arrows began to whistle past them as the Comanches in the forefront of the charge came within range of their bows. Allen lay between Lacey and Eleanora, trying to shield both of them with his body as much as he could, and Antonio did the same with Rico. On the seat, Helen Wayne drove the team with a desperate intensity, knowing that she might be hit at any second. Her eyes searched the trees for an opening big enough to drive the wagon through. She spotted one and yanked the team over, lining them up with it.

The man driving the stagecoach headed the same way, and for a moment, Helen thought the two vehicles were going to collide. She hauled up on the reins, slowing down the wagon, and the coach shot in front of her. She followed it into the trees, bringing the wagon to a shuddering halt.

The people on board left the wagon quickly, diving off to hunt better cover. Allen practically had to carry

Eleanora, but he and Lacey managed to get her off the hides and crouched behind a tree.

As Tucker scanned the plain separating them from the Indians, he saw that all the hunters had made it to safety except one. That one, a man named Parsons, was lying face down, the back of his head blown off by a Comanche bullet. His horse, however, had followed the other horses on into the trees.

The firing continued as the main force of nearly two hundred Indians charged the trees. Tucker had never seen so many Indians in one place. He had fought Indians before but had never encountered anything like this.

Tucker had moved back into the cover of the trees and found a good spot for himself. He sensed movement beside him and looked over to see Lacey dropping down next to him. "What are you doing?" he snapped. "You get farther back in the trees, gal! You want to get yourself shot?"

"I wanted to make sure you were all right," she told him.

"I'm fine. How about you folks on the wagon?"

"None of us were hurt other than some bruises from being bounced around." Lacey ducked as a slug whined close by overhead. "What are we going to do, Tucker?"

The fact that she used his first name was not lost on him, but at the moment there was not time to think about it. "All we can do is hold out as long as we can," he said.

"That's not going to be forever, though, is it?"

He shook his head. "Nope. We can't hold out more than a day or so, I'd say. But we can last that long, easy. There's water here, and we've still got ammunition. That's one good thing about hunting buffalo. You make sure you bring plenty of cartridges for all of your weapons."

"What about one of us going for help?"

"The Comanches would get anybody who tried. Besides, where would you go?"

"Sometimes there are cavalry patrols out here," she told him. "If I could run across one of them . . ."

"You?"

"Well, who did you think I was talking about?" Lacey asked. "I'm a damn good rider. Give me a good mount and I'll outrun those Comanches."

Tucker laughed humorlessly. "I don't think so. No, when we leave here, we'll all leave together."

"Or not leave at all," Lacey pointed out.

"Or not leave at all." Tucker raised up long enough to trigger off a couple of shots. "Still, riding out alone is too big a risk."

Lacey did not say anything in reply to that, and Tucker worried that she would take it in her head to carry out her crazy plan.

"Hadn't you better get back under cover? I reckon you've got that fiancé of yours pretty worried."

"I'm where I want to be," Lacey said. "And I'm not sure he's my fiancé anymore."

Tucker had to glance over at her in response to that comment, and he could tell by the look on her face that she was serious. Allen Kerry had told Tucker that Lacey was really in love with him, and that was more than Tucker ever would have hoped for—but maybe it was true.

This was one hell of a situation in which to fall in love—huddling in a clump of trees in the middle of nowhere, surrounded by a couple of hundred enraged Comanches. . . .

Tucker suddenly realized that he was grinning, that Lacey was smiling back at him. She put out a hand and rested it on his arm for a moment, and in that touch was everything that neither of them had the time to say just then.

The Indians circled the trees for what seemed like days. They could have rushed the group and over-whelmed them by sheer force of numbers, but many warriors would have died in such an attack. The gunfire from the entrenched buffalo hunters was witheringly accurate. Yet by the time the sun was low on the western horizon, six more men had been killed. It was only a matter of time. The Indians could wait them out, picking them off one by one.

Just before the sun slipped out of sight, Tucker's keen eyes spotted one of the Indians sitting his horse on a little ridge over a mile away. It was one of the Comanches, a chieftain, more than likely, and almost certainly the man in charge of the war party. Tucker saw him wave, and abruptly the Indians began to withdraw, pulling back from the circle of trees. They stopped shooting, which made the hunters stop as well. A strange silence fell over the plains, a silence made more eerie by the thunderous violence that had come before.

Burl Wayne came up beside Tucker, his Winchester in his hand. "Wonder what them heathens are up to now?" he growled. "There's got to be a reason they pulled out."

"They're probably letting us think about it," Tucker said. "Reckon they'd like to let us stew all night before they come back and wipe us out in the morning."

Wayne's lip curled in a sneer. "Damn savages. Can't even kill a man and have done with it. I won't stand for it!"

Tucker did not even look at him. "What are you going to do about it?"

Silence was his only answer.

Lacey came up beside Tucker again. During the long afternoon, she had left his side only occasionally, usually to check on Allen and Eleanora and make sure they were all right. She was also worried about Rico Lopez, but the boy seemed to be holding up well, as well as could be expected. He was a brave young man.

Lacey slipped her hand into Tucker's and squeezed. He frowned in surprise, and she was afraid for a moment that she had been too forward. A man like Tucker would not be accustomed to a woman taking his hand like that. But then he smiled and pressed her hand in response, and Lacey knew it was all right. Burl Wayne wandered off to check on the rest of their defenses, such as they were.

Standing there under the trees, hand in hand with Tucker McCall as the sun went down, Lacey thought that despite all the hardships and danger, regardless of the outcome, she was glad her trail had led her to this spot.

No matter what the morning brought, there was still tonight.

Two miles away, Quanah, chief of the Quahadi Comanche, traded glare for glare with the war chief called Bear Running. Bear Running had been furious when his band arrived to find that Quanah and his men were attacking the white men. "I sent word that I was coming to join you," Bear Running said now. "Why did you not wait until I had come before killing the white men?"

"Bear Running is a great warrior and a wise chief," Quanah replied, holding his temper and making an effort to be diplomatic. "But Quanah knows his own mind. We have pursued the white men for two days now. It was time to put an end to this game."

Quanah did not voice the real reason he had ordered his men to attack once more. He had hoped that the white men would keep running, but instead they had taken refuge in the trees.

The reason Quanah wanted the hunters to run was not a simple one, and he did not expect a man like Bear Running to understand it. Deep within Quanah was something different from the other chiefs of the People. He recognized it and hid it away, lest the followers turn on him in misunderstanding.

There was no fiercer warrior than Quanah . . . but he did not want war with the white men.

He wanted the whites gone from the land of the People; in that regard he was in agreement with his brothers. But he knew that war would bring pain and suffering not only to the white men, but also to the Quahadi. The fight would be a long one and not an easy one to win, if indeed winning was possible.

Quanah preferred to harass the white men, to drive them in front of him like cattle out of the Panhandle. Some killing was unavoidable, but he wanted as little blood spilled as possible. If they wiped out the whole

band of buffalo hunters, there would no doubt be an
outcry among the white settlers. The soldiers would
come, and there would be no end to the blood then.
Better to stay behind the hunters, attacking and then
pulling back to keep them moving until they had left
the land of the People. They would have gone anyway,
but this way they had had to pay a price. Perhaps they
would not come back. That was Quanah's hope.

But now Bear Running had arrived, and Quanah
knew that he would stand for nothing less than death
for all the white men. Quanah listened to Bear Running
rant about the evil white invaders and felt his heart
sink.

He was a leader of the People. He could not let a
flea like this Bear Running embarrass him in front of his
followers. With despair in his heart, Quanah heard
himself saying, "I am happy you are here with us, Bear
Running. Tomorrow at dawn we will ride together against
the white men, and together we will kill them."

Overhead, stars began to twinkle into life against
the darkening sky as the whoops of the warriors reached
up to touch the night.

Chapter Nine

The night was almost too quiet, Tucker McCall thought as he peered out at the shadows mantling the plains. The Sharps Big Fifty was at his side as he knelt beside a tree, and the Winchester was in his hand.

Behind him, in the middle of the clump of trees, the hunters had started a fire. There was no point in having a cold camp tonight; the Indians knew where they were. The men were enjoying hot food and coffee for a change, food prepared by Helen and Lacey. Wayne had also allowed them to break out several bottles of whiskey that had been in their saddlebags. Some of the men laughed coarsely and ran their hands over Helen's body as she tried to work at the fire. So far they had left Lacey and Eleanora alone, but it was only a matter of time until they tried to molest the women.

The implications were obvious: *Eat, drink, and be merry . . . for tomorrow you die.*

The quote came back to Tucker from somewhere in the recesses of his memory, maybe from some book his mother had read to him. One thing was certain—it told the story this night.

But if anybody tried to lay hands on Lacey, Tucker would kill him. That was certain, too.

Allen and Eleanora sat together on the ground a little way from the fire, trying to keep some distance between themselves and the rowdy buffalo hunters. Nearby were Antonio and Rico Lopez. Ben Proctor and Willie Morse sat closer to the fire, trying to cut the slight chill that had moved in with the night. Louis Shepherd sat by himself, his face dark and brooding.

Burl Wayne stood back away from the fire a bit, surveying the situation. He knew Tucker was on guard at the edge of the trees and would sound the alarm if the Indians broke with their custom and attacked during the night.

There was a plan in Wayne's head, a desperate plan to be sure, but it was about the only option left to him. He would let the men have their fun for a little while longer. He wanted them to be feeling their liquor enough to boost their courage and diminish their scruples. The time for him to make his move was coming soon.

Tucker heard the carousing around the fire getting wilder and wondered if he should go and make sure that Lacey was all right. But he knew that Allen was there to help her, and the young Easterner would do his part, even though the romance between him and Lacey seemed to be over. Besides, Tucker had the feeling that Lacey could hold her own in a scrap.

From his seat near the fire, Ben Proctor looked up and saw Burl Wayne watching from the shadows under the trees. There was a calculating look on the buffalo hunter's face. Proctor had seen enough of Wayne to know that he was always on the lookout for something to benefit him. Could be Wayne was planning some way to get out of this mess.

Proctor got to his feet and ambled around the camp toward Wayne, ignoring Willie Morse's question of where he was going.

Wayne saw him coming and shifted slightly on his feet, setting himself for trouble if that was what Proctor had in mind.

"Thinkin' about gettin' out of here, ain't you?" Proctor said without preamble.

"What else would anybody be thinkin' about?"

"I been figgerin'. Those Comanches are so sure of themselves, they ain't made any move to surround us. They're just sittin' there to the north, almost like they'd just as soon chase us off as kill us. Well, that may just

be the edge you need. If you was to leave that fire
burnin' and move quiet enough and quick enough, you
might just be able to slip out of here without them
redskins knowin' you're gone."

"Think so?" Wayne replied noncommittally.

"'Course, it might work better if you was to strand
a few folks on foot so they'd slow the Comanches down
in the mornin'."

Wayne moved slightly, just enough to bring the
muzzle of his rifle more in line with Proctor. "You got
somethin' to say, spit it out, mister."

"I'm sayin' I want to go with you," Proctor told
him bluntly. "I know you're plannin' on makin' a run
for it. You got some extra horses now, and I want one of
'em."

Wayne smiled, and it was not a pretty sight in the
red glare from the fire. "Why would I want to do that?"

"I could pay you. I ain't got much with me, but—"

"Any money in the express box in the boot?" Wayne
cut in.

Proctor shook his head. "Don't think I didn't do
some figgerin' about that. But there ain't nothin' in it
but mail."

"Forget it, old man. You ain't got anything I want.
Those hides are all I'm worryin' about."

"What about *our* hides?" Proctor asked angrily.
"Ain't they worth anything?"

"Not to me. Now go back and sit down."

Proctor went back to the fire with his face set in
furious lines. Burl Wayne was going to abandon him
out here with the others. And this time, those on foot
would not be allowed to straggle along behind.

Meanwhile, Wayne made his way around the fire
toward Tucker's position. He had decided not to wait
any longer. The only real opposition he anticipated
would come from Tucker McCall, and Wayne was going
to be ready for that.

Tucker heard movement behind him and turned
his head. "McCall!" he heard Burl Wayne say, and then
he spotted Wayne's diminutive figure in the shadows.
Wayne beckoned to him, calling him in toward the fire.

Tucker hesitated and then decided to go see what Wayne wanted. He picked up the Sharps in his left hand and strode the few feet to the fire.

"What is it?" he asked.

In reply, Wayne's hand dipped toward his waist. Tucker saw the movement and knew what was about to happen, but Wayne was too quick for him to do anything about it.

Wayne had the big Remington out, its muzzle lined on Tucker's body almost before anyone knew what was happening. A sudden silence fell around the campfire.

"I don't want any trouble from you, McCall," Wayne began. "But we're gettin' out of here, and I ain't gonna let you stop us."

"What the hell are you talking about, Wayne? Have you forgotten there's a couple of hundred Comanches out there?" Tucker asked dryly.

"I ain't forgettin' anything, especially the way you been runnin' your mouth the last few days, McCall. The Indians are north of here. The way south is still clear."

"Now how can you be sure of that?" Tucker exploded.

"Them Indians have been chasin' us for two days. I know what direction they're comin' from. And after the last attack, they pulled back to the north again." Wayne raised his voice slightly. "Listen, you men. You do like I say, and you'll live to spend your money in the Dodge City whorehouses! But we got to get out of here tonight."

"You mean make a run for it?" one of the hunters asked. "Are we gonna forget those damn buffalo hides and save our own damn hides?"

"We ain't leavin' the hides," Wayne said. "We've got extra horses now. We'll hitch a couple more to the wagon and the coach, and we can make a lot better time."

"Won't the Injuns know we're gone?" another hunter asked.

"Not if we leave somebody here to keep them busy. We ain't takin' any pilgrims with us this time."

"You mean to leave these people here, Wayne?"
Tucker demanded angrily.

"That's right. I figure they'll at least slow down
them Indians when they attack in the mornin'."

Allen Kerry was on his feet. "You can't do that!" he
exclaimed. "It would be pure murder to leave us here.
Besides, what's to stop us from coming along on foot as
we've been doing?"

Wayne kept his gun pointed at Tucker, but the
threat was plain enough in his voice as he replied, "*I'll*
stop you. I'll shoot anybody who comes after us, Indian
or white." He grinned arrogantly. "And anyway, with
the extra horses we'll be goin' a lot faster than a walk
this time. So you folks can stay here in the trees and
wait for the Comanches, or you can go out and meet
them. Up to you."

"You bastard," Tucker said.

"Never claimed to be anything but," Wayne said.
"You can't hurt my feelin's, McCall. All I know is I'm
gettin' out of this alive, and with them buffalo hides."
He looked around at the hunters. "Are you men with
me?"

For a long moment, there was silence. Then one of
the hunters stood up and said, "Reckon I ain't ready to
cash in just yet. I'm with you, Wayne." A few more
nodded, and then gradually all of them murmured their
assent. They weren't proud of what they were about to
do, but all of them wanted to live. And they had con-
sumed just enough liquor to give them the bravado to
believe they could make good their escape with the
valuable hides in tow.

Tucker McCall, ready to burst from anger, fought
to control his temper as Wayne ordered five of his men
to hold their rifles on the passengers while he relieved
them of their weapons. Tucker wanted to reach for the
hilt of his bowie knife, which Wayne had not seen. But
Wayne did not even give him the instant he would
need to get it out. Tucker could see that the little man's
finger was taut on the trigger of the Remington.

After the weapons had been taken, Lacey went to
Allen and Eleanora and stood with them. She was cast-

ing about frantically in her mind for something she
could do to stop this. She thought about the Colt still
hidden in the waistband of her jeans. Wayne would not
expect her to be armed. She could slip the pistol out
and shoot him, and he would never know what had hit
him.

But could she kill a man in cold blood like that?
Even a man as low as Burl Wayne?

If she did not, it might mean that Tucker would
get shot instead. She knew that Wayne was just waiting
for one wrong move on Tucker's part.

Her fingers edged toward the butt of the Colt.

Proctor, Willie, and the others were on their feet
as well. Willie said urgently, "Ben, we've got to do
something!"

"Ain't much we *can* do, kid," Proctor growled.
"Wayne's got the whip hand."

"We've got to move quiet," Burl Wayne was saying
to his men. "The Comanche may be watchin' us. But
we got to take the chance. Once we're away from here a
little ways, we'll pour on the speed. By mornin', we'll
be a long way from here. Now, get ready to roll."

Wayne stood with his pistol covering Tucker while
the other hunters hitched up the teams to the wagon
and the coach.

Helen stood slightly apart from the activity, her
face showing the strain she felt. Lacey Ellis had become
her friend; she did not want to go off and leave the
woman to die. It might not do any good, but she had to
say *something*. . . .

"Don't do this, Burl," she began, stepping closer
to him. "These people never did anything to hurt you.
We'll have some extra horses now, even after hitching
some of them up. Can't they double up on those?"

Wayne shook his head stubbornly. "We may need
extra mounts."

Lacey spoke up, her voice cool. "He's really doing
it to be cruel, Helen. That's the way he is."

"You shut up, bitch," Wayne cursed.

Tucker tensed at Wayne's insult to Lacey, but he
made an effort to keep hold of his temper. He was still

hoping to find some way to turn things around, to get all of them out safely.

"Don't talk to her that way, Burl," Helen said. "She's my friend."

Wayne grinned nastily. "Reckon all you ladies are friends. Well, that gives me an idea. Maybe we can spare a couple of extra horses after all. We'll just take the women along. . . ."

Hope began to spring up on Helen's face.

"And then when we get out of this, you boys can have 'em," Wayne finished. "Reckon they'll be so glad to be alive, they'll be right grateful."

"Goddamn you!" Tucker exploded. He saw the leering grins on the faces of the hunters, knew what would be in store for Lacey and Eleanora under those circumstances. He could not allow that to happen.

If he could just get his hands on Wayne, even if Wayne killed him . . .

Lacey felt cold horror go through her at Wayne's words and knew she could not wait any longer. She had her fingers wrapped around the Colt's butt, and she slid it out, lifting it, tipping the barrel toward the unsuspecting Burl Wayne.

The movement was enough to attract Ben Proctor's attention. In that second, he saw in Lacey's Colt his only opportunity to get out of this mess alive—by forcing Wayne to take him along or by killing the greedy little man. But first he had to take possession of the gun.

He lunged forward and reached for the gun, hoping to grab it from her hand before she had a chance to fire it. Lacey cried out and tried to wrench the weapon free from Proctor's grip.

Tucker's eyes darted away from Wayne to check on what was happening to Lacey, and Wayne grabbed his chance. He leaped at Tucker, lashing out at him with the pistol. The barrel slammed into Tucker's head as he tried to grab the bowie knife from its sheath on his hip.

The blow staggered him, and the knife slipped from his fingers even as he yanked it free. He surged ahead into Wayne, wrapping his arms around the smaller

man and lifting him off his feet. Tucker began applying
pressure in the bear hug and took a couple of steps one
way, then the other. His brain was spinning from the
blow on the head, and he knew he had to clear it if he
was going to be able to hold on to the frantically struggling Wayne.

By now Ben Proctor had Lacey's gun in his hand,
but she was keeping him too occupied to use it. She
was attacking him with her fists, pounding on his chest,
until he managed to get her in a bear hug, still holding
the gun securely in his hand. She squirmed and fought
like a wildcat to get free, but Proctor reached up and
tangled the fingers of his free hand in her hair, jerking
her head back, then took the butt of the gun and
slammed it across her jaw, snapping her head around
and making her go limp in Proctor's arms.

Burl Wayne fought for breath as Tucker tried to
crush the life from him, and no one moved to help him.
This was his fight to win or lose. His face pulled back in
a grimace of pain, Wayne lifted the pistol again and put
all his strength into a savage slash at Tucker's head.

The barrel of Wayne's gun thudded against Tucker's skull, cushioned some by his hat, but still he groaned
as pain blasted through him. He felt his grip on Wayne
slipping away, but there was nothing he could do to
stop it.

Tucker slumped to the ground, out cold.

Gasping for breath, Wayne glanced over at Proctor, who was still holding the stunned Lacey and her
Colt.

"What about it?" Proctor demanded, pointing the
gun toward Wayne. "Reckon savin' your life is worth a
place on one of them extra horses? Or do I have to
shoot you?"

Catching his breath, Wayne nodded. "Reckon you
can drive the coach. Probably make better time with a
regular driver at the reins, anyway. Duffy'll go along to
ride shotgun and spell you, if you need it." He glared
down at Tucker and swung the pistol toward him. "Now
for this son of a bitch."

"Don't do it, Burl!"

Helen Wayne's voice cut through the night. It carried conviction, and when her brother looked up in surprise, he saw that she was holding a Winchester leveled in his direction. "What the hell do you think you're doin'?" he asked incredulously.

"Tucker's knocked out. He can't stop you now. There's no need for more killin'."

Wayne smirked. "The Indians'll just do it in the mornin'."

"Maybe so, but you ain't gonna do it."

"Yeah, Wayne," one of the hunters put in. "And the noise might rouse them Injuns."

Another hunter stepped forward and added, "Also, Tucker'll help slow 'em down tomorrow."

"All right," Wayne said disgustedly. He rammed his pistol back into its holster. "Let's get movin', you men. We're wastin' time!"

As the hunters continued their preparation to leave, Tucker remained where he had fallen, insensible. Helen kept the rifle handy, watching Wayne, but he did not make any further attempt to harm Tucker. In fact, he seemed to have forgotten about Tucker McCall in the press of getting ready to pull out.

Proctor held on to Lacey until one of the hunters took her and got her aboard a horse. Lacey was still groggy and did not seem fully aware of what was going on. Proctor was watching Willie Morse, who was regarding him in disbelief.

"You can't help these . . . these bastards, Ben," Willie said. "You just can't."

"Sorry, Willie," Proctor said, though he did not sound regretful. "But I reckon I am one of these bastards now. Maybe I always was. I'd try to bring you along, kid," he added almost as an afterthought, "but I'm afraid you'd have a different story of what happened than I plan to tell."

One of the hunters came over to get Eleanora, but she shrank away from him and let out a scream. "Shut your mouth," he growled, grabbing her arm roughly.

Allen tried to hit the man, but the hunter dodged him easily and swung a blow of his own. His fist knocked

Allen backward, and a kick to the stomach sent him sprawling.

"You best stay down, mister," the hunter told him, then dragged the screaming and struggling Eleanora to one of the horses.

"Knock her out and tie her on the saddle if she don't shut up," Wayne told the man, and that threat made Eleanora quiet down somewhat. The hunter boosted her into the saddle, obviously enjoying the way he planted his meaty hand against her backside. She slumped there in the saddle, sobbing softly.

Louis Shepherd watched her being manhandled and told himself he ought to do something about it. He cared for the woman, and here he was standing by while she was mistreated and kidnapped.

What could he do, though, except get himself killed that much sooner? All his plans were ashes now, his life something that could probably be measured in hours. What importance did anything he did have now?

Allen turned imploringly to Helen. "Can't you do something?" he asked.

Fighting back tears, Helen bit her lip and said, "I kept Burl from killing Tucker. And I'll watch out for Lacey and your sister. I'm sorry, Allen, but that's all I can do."

"I suppose all the things we talked about meant nothing to you," he said bitterly. "I was going to take you to Boston."

Pain showed on Helen's face as she said, "It meant a lot to me, Allen. You were a heap nicer to me than any man ever has been before. But I can't stop Burl short of killin' him, and I can't do that. Oh, God, I am sorry."

Allen was silent for a moment. Then he said, "I know. And if this means that you and Lacey and Eleanora will live, then that's what I want. Be careful, Helen."

She nodded. "I will. Maybe we'll meet again someday, Allen. I hope so."

"Yes. Perhaps we will."

The hunters were mounting up, with Ben Proctor taking his place atop the coach. At the last moment,

Burl Wayne changed his mind about having Duffy ride shotgun and told him to drive the other wagon in Helen's place. It was clear that he no longer trusted his sister—not after she had leveled a rifle at him.

Lacy was regaining her senses now, but it was too late for her to do anything about her predicament. Her hands were lashed to the pommel of the saddle, as were Eleanora's. Looking back at her fellow stagecoach passengers, Lacey's breath caught in her throat as she spotted Tucker's body lying on the ground, and for one horrible moment she thought Wayne had killed him. Then, in the uneven glow of the firelight, she thought she saw his chest rise and fall.

She did not look closer. She would cling to the hope that Tucker was alive. He *had* to be alive. Because as long as Tucker McCall was alive, she had a chance to escape. He would come for her . . . somehow.

Allen had gotten to his feet. He stood holding his stomach where he had been kicked, his face twisted in anger and despair. He turned to Willie Morse and said, "We've got to do something!"

Willie was looking at Ben Proctor up on the coach. "Don't reckon there's much we can do, Mr. Kerry. Some folks don't give a damn about anything. They'd shoot anybody who got in their way." His voice was tinged with bitterness. Proctor had always been a grouchy old coot, but they had been partners. And that was supposed to count for something.

Allen started toward the hunters, but Antonio Lopez reached out and put a hand on his arm, stopping him. "There is nothing you can do, señor, except get yourself killed."

"What difference does it make?" Allen flared at him. "The Indians will come back in the morning and do it then."

"We must not give up hope." Antonio's other hand was on Rico's shoulder, and it tightened now. "I have taught my son that all things are possible with faith. I have not given up my faith."

The vaquero's calming words reached Allen somehow, and he took a deep breath. "I'm going to see how Tucker is," he said.

As Allen knelt beside Tucker's motionless form, Burl Wayne called out, "Your weapons and ammo will be waitin' for you less than a quarter mile away. You should be able to see where we drop 'em off the wagon." He grinned evilly at the men. "I wouldn't want to leave you unable to defend yourselves when them Comanches attack tomorrow mornin'. You'll do a good job of holdin' 'em off, so we can gain some distance, won't you?"

With a hollow laugh, Wayne waved his men into motion, and the wagon and coach, with the extra horses added to their teams, got started with a creak of wheels.

Within moments, the party had left the small circle of light from the campfire, and minutes later the stranded men could faintly make out the shape of the wagon as it halted long enough to drop the guns. After that, they could hear the riders pick up speed, and then the sounds of their passage quickly faded into the night. The six people left in the trees might have been the only ones in a hundred miles, to judge by the silence.

Allen checked for a pulse in Tucker's neck and found a strong one. There was a gash in the big man's scalp where Wayne had hit him with the pistol, but the bleeding had already stopped. Tucker would have a hell of a headache when he woke up, but he would probably be all right.

At least until dawn.

Allen and Willie set off in the darkness to the spot where the weapons had been dumped. The others waited silently for their return, afraid that the sounds of Wayne and his hunters had alerted the Indians. But the two men returned unscathed, and the guns were heaped near the fire.

Minutes later, Tucker McCall began to groan and move slightly. He opened his eyes, wincing as the glare from the fire struck them, and then tried to sit up. Allen reached out to help him, but Tucker shook off his hand. "I can do it," he muttered, then realized that Allen was only trying to help him. "Sorry."

"That's all right. How's your head?"

Tucker lifted a hand and gingerly touched the wound. "Feels like a herd of buffalo stampeded through it. What happened?"

"Wayne clouted you with his gun," Willie put in.

"I heard Lacey yell. . . ."

"She had gotten hold of a gun somehow," Allen said, sounding as if he had a hard time believing it. "She tried to shoot Wayne, but Ben Proctor stopped her before she could fire."

"Proctor? Where is he?"

"He left with the hunters," Shepherd said. "Wayne decided to let him drive the coach."

Tucker hauled himself slowly to his feet and looked around the fire. "Where are the women?"

"Wayne and the others, they took them," Allen said, his voice thick. "I tried to stop them, but—"

"I'm going to kill Burl Wayne," Tucker said simply. He bent over, scooped up his hat, and started to put it on. He changed his mind when he felt the pain it caused his head wound; he flung the hat away. "Where's my horse?" he demanded.

"They took it, too," Willie told him. "I saw one of the hunters leading it. We're stuck here, Mr. McCall."

"And they're moving too quickly now for us to catch up on foot," Shepherd put in. "It's all over, McCall. There's no way out for us."

"We'll see about that." Though his head was pounding and his legs felt a little weak, Tucker's natural leadership began to assert itself. "How are we fixed for weapons?"

Willie Morse told Tucker about retrieving the guns and walked over to the pile and hefted his shotgun, which he had kept near him since being thrown off the coach. "I've got this shotgun and my six-gun, but not many rounds for either of them."

Shepherd picked up the little pocket pistol from the pile and said, "This is the only gun I've got, I'm afraid."

Allen picked up the Colt that Lacey had pulled on Wayne. "This is the one Lacey got ahold of."

Tucker turned to Antonio. "How about you, amigo?"

"Nothing, I am afraid."

"Can you use a handgun?"

"*Sí*," Antonio nodded.

Tucker bent over and retrieved his own holster and then slipped his Colt out of it. "I never was much count with one. Here, you can use this."

"I can shoot a rifle," Rico said. He was scared, but he felt a kinship with these men, even though he was only a little boy. He wanted to make his father and Señor Tucker proud of him. He would not cry, no matter what came.

"Don't think we've got enough to go around, son, but I'll keep that in mind," Tucker told him.

The situation was bleak, and Tucker knew it. They did not have enough firepower to hold the Indians off for long, but the only alternative was to leave the cover of the trees. They could not get far enough on foot during the night to escape the Indians, and the Comanches would kill them out of hand if they were caught in the open. Staying in the trees represented a very faint hope, but it was the only hope.

"We'd better get some sleep," Tucker told the little group. "I'll stand the first watch."

"Wake me in a couple of hours," Willie said. Allen and Antonio also offered to stand watches. Shepherd was withdrawn and said nothing, simply walking over to a tree, sitting down, and leaning against the trunk.

The others followed his example, all except Tucker, who went to the edge of the trees and fastened his gaze on the spot where the Indians had disappeared earlier.

He knew that there would not be much sleeping tonight, if any. Time was too precious now, when all they had left were the hours until dawn. Tucker heard a soft murmur of voices from Antonio and Rico and knew that the father and son had much to talk about. This had to be a bittersweet moment for them. Only recently had they lost their wife and mother, and now they were going to lose their own lives. But at least they were facing the end together.

Maybe dying was a little easier if you were with someone you loved. Until the last few days, Tucker had always figured he would die friendless and alone. But that was before he met Lacey Ellis. Now he wished he had had the chance to tell her more about the way he felt for her. He wished she was at his side so that he could take her into his arms and let her know that he loved her.

Wherever she was, she knew. That was Tucker's prayer as he waited to die. And he prayed for her safety, as well. It had been a long time since he prayed for anything, and now tonight he suddenly found that he was praying for all sorts of things. It was a habit a man could get into, he supposed.

There was a rustle of movement behind him. Tucker looked back and saw a figure looming out of the darkness. He tensed for a moment in anticipation of trouble, but then he recognized the shape of Allen Kerry.

"What are you doing here?" Tucker asked. "Your watch isn't for hours yet."

Allen shook his head. "I couldn't sleep. I don't think any of the others can, either. We all know what's going to happen in the morning, even little Rico. There were some things I wanted to say to you."

"I'm listening."

Taking a deep breath, Allen said, "This is your land, McCall, not mine. You belong out here, and I never should have come. I respect you, though. You proved to me that everyone in the West isn't like Burl Wayne." He paused for a moment and then went on, "I think Lacey saw the goodness in you right away."

Such talk made Tucker uncomfortable. "You don't have to say anything else," he muttered.

"Yes, I do. I know you don't need my blessing for anything you do, and I wouldn't be so presumptuous as to try to give it. I just want you to know that I realize Lacey and I weren't as well matched as we thought. She needed a different kind of man than I would ever want to be. I'm sorry you and she didn't get a chance to find out if you were that man."

Tucker did not look at Allen; he kept his eyes on the plains washed by starlight and the glow of a half-moon. After a few seconds of silence, he said, "Might

be you're more of a man than you think, friend. You
may be a fish out of water around here, but damned if
you don't try most of the time."

Allen chuckled softly. "Thanks. Don't get the idea
I want to stay out here, though. Good Lord, I wish I
was in Boston right now."

"You know something, pard? So do I."

Both men laughed, and then Allen said, "One of
my regrets is that I didn't get to know Helen Wayne
any better. It seemed to me that there were the mak-
ings of a remarkable individual there."

"I reckon so," Tucker agreed. "When I first saw
the two of you talking, I was worried that you'd treat
her bad, like the rest of Wayne's bunch. Figured out
after a while that you really liked her."

"She wanted to go back east and perhaps get some
schooling. That seemed to me an honorable goal, and I
wanted to help her achieve it. It's a pity things didn't
work out that way."

"There aren't many second chances in this life,"
Tucker said. "Sometimes there aren't even any first
chances. Like for Rico. The little feller didn't hardly
have time to get his eyes good and open."

"We should be praying for a miracle, I suppose."

"Most times out here, a miracle comes out of the
barrel of a gun." Tucker grunted. "But a little prayer
can't hurt."

"Well, regardless of what happens in the morning,
I'm glad we had this talk tonight." Allen stuck out his
hand. "And I'm glad you and I met, Tucker McCall."

Tucker hesitated only an instant before he took
Allen's hand and returned the grip. "Same here."

It looked like it was going to be a beautiful day,
Tucker thought as the sun rose. The air was crisp and
cool, and the only clouds were high, fleecy wisps. When
you breathed deep, you could almost taste how sweet
life was. There was nothing like early morning on the
high plains.

Especially when you were about to die . . .

They all stood near the edge of the trees. Tucker

was in the middle of the group. Antonio Lopez was to his right, with Allen Kerry on the other side of Antonio. To Tucker's left stood Willie Morse, with Louis Shepherd on the end. Behind them, several feet back in the trees, was Rico Lopez.

In front of them, several hundred yards away, were the Comanches, massed on the plains and ready to charge.

Tucker had watched all night and had seen no sign of the Indians going around them. Maybe Burl Wayne's plan had worked, at least for now. The Indians were not going to be delayed here for long, though, and as soon as they discovered that there were only a handful of white men here, they would be off again in pursuit of the main group.

With any luck, Wayne and the others would reach Adobe Walls before the Indians could catch up. Maybe Lacey would live. And Tucker was willing to lay odds that she would find some way to get away from the hunters before they had a chance to molest her.

Tucker was going to sell his own life at as high a price as possible. It was all he could do now for Lacey.

War whoops came drifting through the morning air, and dust began to puff upward.

"Here they come, boys," Tucker said quietly. He raised the Big Fifty to his shoulder. "Let's give 'em a warm welcome."

The other men lifted their weapons. They waited. One minute went by, then two, and still they waited. The Indians were close now, a hundred yards, seventy-five, fifty . . .

Tucker squeezed the trigger of his Sharps, and hell erupted. Gunfire blasted from the men in the trees and was returned by the Indians. Several of the Comanche ponies faltered and fell, their riders going headlong. But that was not enough to blunt the charge. This time there would be no circling of the trees, no harassing and sniping. This time the Indians would overrun them, guiding the horses skillfully through the trees and wiping out the hated white men.

Tucker had dropped the Sharps after the first shot

and had taken up the Winchester, firing as fast as he could, pouring slugs into the charging Comanches. He would not have time to reload, but when the rifle was empty, there was always the bowie. It would be good for a bloody few minutes.

Antonio Lopez held Tucker's Colt steady in his hand and fired methodically until it was empty. He had extra shells in his other hand, and he quickly snapped open the cylinder and began plugging in the fresh bullets. He felt a hand clutch at his leg and looked down to see Rico standing there, looking up with his frightened little face.

"I want to be with you, Papa!" the boy cried, and Antonio's heart broke. He had wanted only what was best for his son, and now they would both die. He knelt, slipped an arm around Rico, and hugged him hard. Then he closed the cylinder of the Colt, turned to face the Indians again, and said, "Stay behind me, Rico." He lifted the gun and squeezed off one shot.

Pain slammed him in the chest. He looked down, saw the shaft of the arrow protruding from his body, and then a wave of blackness washed over him. "Rico . . ." he murmured. Then he slipped down on his back at the feet of his son.

Allen saw Antonio Lopez die and screamed, "Nooo, dammit!" He fired his last shot from the Colt that Lacey had dropped and then fell to his knees next to Rico, reaching out to enfold the horror-struck boy in his arms. He held Rico and waited for the end.

Willie Morse emptied his own six-gun and then lifted the shotgun. He would have to wait until the Indians got closer, but at least a couple of the Comanches were going to get one hell of a surprise.

At the end of the line, Louis Shepherd heard the click as the hammer of his pistol fell on an empty chamber. He looked up and saw the fierce expressions on the faces of the Indians. He read his own death there, and something in his mind snapped. Dropping the pistol, he charged out of the trees, screaming.

Before he had taken ten steps, he pitched forward on his face, his body riddled with arrows. As his fingers scrabbled feebly in the dirt, tears came to his eyes, but they were not tears of pain.

All his life, he had wanted something better for himself. And this was how it ended; all his plans, all his schemes, had come to nothing.

Tucker McCall saw Shepherd die and knew that within minutes he would be passing over the divide himself. Oddly enough, the notion did not particularly frighten him. He was no hero; he had been scared plenty of times in the past. But it would not do to go out crying.

He dropped the empty Winchester and slid the bowie knife out of its sheath. He grinned, grinned right at the Indian leading the charge. Tucker could see his ugly, howling face now.

The Comanche flew off the back of the horse with a spray of blood, tumbling lifelessly to the hard ground. The next man went down, too, then the next.

It took a minute for Tucker to realize that the booming he now heard came from buffalo guns.

Then he saw what was happening. Buckskin-clad men on fast horses were sweeping in from both sides, peppering the Indians with handgun and rifle fire. More men fired the Big Fifties from a long distance, the heavy slugs cutting a deadly swath through the Comanches. They were buffalo hunters, all right, but not the hunters who had gone with Burl Wayne. Tucker saw them but did not quite believe they were there.

The backbone of the Indian charge was broken within seconds. Trapped in a crossfire, the Comanches did the only thing they could. They split their forces to sweep around the trees and then raced their horses to the south, away from the deadly fire of the newcomers.

Tucker watched them go and dropped a hand on Allen's shoulder. "Reckon we prayed us up a miracle after all," he said.

It was a miracle that had come too late for Antonio Lopez and Louis Shepherd.

In the welter of dust and powder smoke, it had been hard to tell what was happening at first, but now Tucker saw that a party of buffalo hunters some thirty

strong had arrived just in time to save them. Some of
the hunters were firing after the Comanches to keep
them going. These men fought as if there were ten
times their number and yelled like banshees in the
process. The Comanches would be plenty disgusted if
they ever figured out they had been run off by a much
smaller force.

By then Tucker intended to be long gone from
here.

Allen stood up and carried Rico with him as he
joined Tucker and Willie. They strode from the trees to
meet two of the buffalo hunters who were riding toward
them.

"Looks like you ran into a little trouble, friend,"
one of the men said as they reined up. He dropped
down out of the saddle and extended a hand. "Name's
Masterson, Bat Masterson. Hope we got here in time."

Tucker shook hands with Masterson. The man was
medium sized and rather mild looking, despite the
rough clothes he wore and the rifle he carried. There
was an intensity in his sharp eyes, though, that would
warn anyone who knew how to look for the signs of a
dangerous man.

"We lost a couple," Tucker said simply. "I'm Tucker
McCall. This is Willie Morse and Allen Kerry. The
little fella's Rico Lopez. His pa is back there in the
trees. He's one of the ones we lost."

Masterson nodded gravely. "I'm sorry, Rico," he
said to the boy. "We came as soon as we heard the
shooting." He turned to indicate the other man, who
was solid looking and wore a dark, drooping mustache
that made him appear older than his years. "This here
is Billy Dixon, my partner. We're heading up this
bunch."

Tucker shook hands with Billy Dixon. "Heard your
name mentioned a time or two," he said.

"I've heard of you, too, McCall. Thought you were
still up in Kansas."

"The buffalo are down here now." Tucker shrugged,
and Dixon nodded in understanding.

"We'd heard that the Comanches were in an uproar," Masterson said. "So when the shooting started, it was pretty easy to figure that somebody was in trouble. We split up so we could come in from two sides and then got here as soon as we could." He looked into the trees and frowned. "You don't have any horses. What in tarnation are you doing afoot?"

"We were set afoot on purpose," Tucker said grimly. He saw the sudden anger on Masterson's face. Setting a man afoot was one of the worst crimes that could be committed out here. Quickly, Tucker explained what had happened in the last two days.

"They headed south for Adobe Walls?" Masterson asked. "That's the way those Indians went when they took off from here."

Tucker nodded. "I know. Those Comanches were moving fast, and they're bound to be pretty mad about being run off. I think we should try to catch up to them, if you can spare some horses for us to ride."

"We can spare 'em. Billy, round up the boys and tell 'em we're riding after those Comanches."

Dixon grinned, the expression giving his solemn face a certain fierceness. "I'll tell 'em, Bat."

As Dixon spurred away, Masterson nodded toward the bodies of Antonio and Shepherd. "We'll have to take those men with us. There's no time to bury them."

Tucker thought about Lacey and Eleanora being in the hands of Wayne's men and about the Indians on their trail. "I think that's the way they'd want it," he said.

Chapter Ten

If the pace Burl Wayne had set before was brutal, the one he pushed them at now was sheer hell. Once the group was well away from the trees, Wayne had yelled for them to speed up, and soon the horses were galloping. The wagon and the coach were hard put to keep up with the riders, and both Ben Proctor and the man handling the reins on the wagon used their whips mercilessly, determined to reach safety or run themselves to death in the attempt.

Even with her hands tied, Lacey was able to handle her horse fairly well. Eleanora had trouble, though, and was reduced to hanging on for dear life. Lacey tried to stay near her, to help if she could.

By the time the sun came up, Burl Wayne was starting to feel more confident. The clump of trees was miles behind them now, so far behind that they could not even hear the shooting as the Indians launched their final massacre. Wayne just hoped that Tucker McCall and the others would put up enough of a fight to slow the Comanches down for a little while. But he could not count on that. Their only real safety lay in reaching Adobe Walls. Despite the exhaustion of men and horses, they had to keep pushing to the south.

About an hour after sunrise, when Burl Wayne pulled up next to the coach, Ben Proctor said from the box, "This country's startin' to look familiar. I think I been through here before the stage route was changed."

"You know how far we are from Adobe Walls?" Wayne asked.

"Quite a ways yet. We ought to be runnin' up on one of them abandoned stations sometime this mornin', though."

That was good to know, Wayne thought. In case the Indians did catch up, there might be a place where they could make a stand.

But making a stand was not good enough. That would just delay the inevitable. A clean getaway was the only thing Burl Wayne wanted.

He turned and gestured for one of the hunters to ride closer. "You there, Gentry," he called. "Drop back and check our back trail!"

The hunter named Gentry looked dubious. "You're sendin' me right into them Injuns, boss."

"Not that far back, you damn fool! Just far enough to see if there's any dust back there. Then hightail it back up here to me. Got that?"

Gentry nodded. "Don't know if my horse has that much left in him, Burl, but I'll give 'er a try." He wheeled the animal around and headed for the rear of the group.

Lacey and Eleanora were riding in the middle of the bunch. Eleanora was sobbing hysterically, and though Lacey tried to talk to her over the pounding of hooves, her words did not seem to be getting through. Too much had happened too quickly. Eleanora had been protected and pampered all her life, first by her family and then by her husband. Until now.

Lacey wished there was something she could say that would console Eleanora. This trip to Texas had been her idea, and she felt some guilt over involving Allen and Eleanora.

Allen . . . Right now he was probably lying back there dead or, worse, was still alive and a captive of the Indians. Lacey prayed fervently that that had not happened.

She knew that the Indians would not have taken Tucker alive. He would have gone down fighting, with a pile of dead Comanches at his feet. In the back of her mind the hope still lingered that he had gotten away, that he would be coming after them. But that would take a miracle.

In all likelihood, she would have to kill Burl Wayne herself.

On the wagon seat beside Duffy, Helen held on tightly to keep from being thrown off. At this rate, the wagon would rattle itself apart before they ever reached Adobe Walls, yet she knew her brother would not consider slowing down. She watched one of the hunters, a man called Gentry, riding back the way they had come and guessed that he was going to check their back trail. She had often looked behind, but the wagon had been raising so much dust that it was hard to tell if anything was back there.

Helen was afraid, but the source of her fear was as much Burl Wayne as it was the Indians. She had seen the way he looked at her when she had held her rifle on him. She doubted that he would go so far as to kill her, but assuming they lived through this, he would do his best to make her life miserable. He was not a forgiving man, and he damn sure would not forget. Yet there really was not much else he could do to her. He already had her cooking and driving the wagon and whoring. How much lower could he force her?

Knowing her brother as well as she did, she was confident that he would come up with something.

By midmorning, a hot sun was beating down. This was going to be another scorcher, at least for this time of year. The heat did not make things any easier for the fleeing group.

Burl Wayne was starting to get worried again. Gentry had not returned, and it should not have taken him this long to check their back trail. Of course, his horse could have given out, as hard as it had been ridden. Or it could have stepped in a prairie-dog hole.

Or the Comanches could have gotten him.

Wayne could not stand the uncertainty. "Keep moving! Keep moving!" he yelled at the men closest to him. Then he turned his horse and galloped toward the rear.

Lacey saw him riding in her direction and wished

she still had her Colt. It would have been simple to pick him off with it. He thundered past, and Lacey looked back over her shoulder at him, wondering what was going on.

Helen saw him, too, and guessed that he was going back to see if something had happened to Gentry. She knew she had not seen the hunter return, and she was afraid that Wayne had sent the man to his death.

Death had ridden with them ever since they left Kansas, Helen thought. It was as though Wayne attracted it with his greed and stubbornness.

Wayne slowed down as he left the group, letting it pull away from him. Their passage had kicked up quite a bit of dust. He rode through it, letting the wind carry it away, and looked for any place that was higher than the surrounding terrain. He found a slight rise within minutes.

There were a pair of Army field glasses in his saddlebag, won in a poker game with a drunken lieutenant in Dodge. Wayne took out the glasses and trained them on the horizon. There was dust there, and he did not like the looks of it. Then he scanned the midground and saw what looked like the bodies of a horse and man, both riddled with arrows.

"Gentry," he muttered, the breath catching in his throat. The Indians were coming, all right.

Wayne cursed and jerked his horse around, putting the spurs to it and racing back toward the others. He felt his heart pounding with fear and anger.

He used his spurs cruelly, trying to urge every bit of speed out of his mount. The animal was half dead—all the horses were—but it responded gamely. Wayne steadily cut the distance between himself and the rest of the group. When he pulled within earshot, he began yelling that the Indians were behind them again.

Wayne pulled up even with the stagecoach. "Where's that way station?" he shouted at Ben Proctor.

Proctor pointed southwest. "Over that way a couple of miles!" he replied. "Leastways, it is if we come up on a dry creek pretty soon! If we don't, reckon I'm lost after all!"

"Come on!" Wayne angled his horse in the direction Proctor had pointed. If the stage driver was wrong about the way station, they were as good as dead.

The dust boiling up from the Indian ponies was easily visible now, but few of the fleeing group glanced behind. They did not need the sight to goad them on, and at this breakneck speed, they had to watch where they were going.

The dry creek bed that Proctor had mentioned appeared up ahead. It was shallow, and its banks were so gradual that the horses and the vehicles had no trouble. The coach and the wagon bounced a bit more than usual, but the hides were tied down securely. Helen and the drivers hung on.

Lacey thought the ride had been wild before, but now it got worse. She wished her hands were untied so that she could keep the horse under better control. Glancing over quickly at Eleanora, Lacey felt a surge of fear. The older woman was swaying in the saddle; if she toppled off the horse, she would be trampled to death by the other riders.

"Hang on, Eleanora!" Lacey urged, but she did not know if Eleanora heard her or not.

Slowly, Burl Wayne's horse pulled ahead of the others, putting him once more in the lead. His mount was a bit fresher than the others, since it had less weight to carry, but it would drop soon at this pace. So would the others.

Wayne saw something up ahead. At first he could not make it out, but then he recognized the ruins for what they were. "There's the way station!" he cried out. "Head for those walls!"

The roof of the adobe building had long since collapsed, taking some of the walls with it, but what was left formed a ragged battlement ranging between three and five feet tall on three sides. The fourth side had a big gap in it, but that was lucky—it would provide an entrance for the wagon and the coach. A few wooden poles were standing upright in the ground several yards from the building, apparently the remains of what had been a corral.

The Indians were in sight now and were firing their rifles at the hunters who lagged behind on the weariest horses. But, fortunately, the range was still too great for the shots to be effective.

Wayne was the first one through the gap. He left his horse in a leap, taking his Sharps and his rifle with him. Crouching behind one of the walls, he lined his sights on the Indians as the other hunters poured into the rough shelter. They dropped down from their saddles and ran to the walls to join Wayne. As the coach and the wagon pulled into the ruins, Wayne looked at the men flanking him and roared, "Give 'em hell!"

The hunters fired, most of them using the big buffalo rifles, resting the heavy muzzles on the walls. The volley tore into the oncoming Indians and sent several warriors plunging from their horses. But the charge was blunted only for a moment.

Somehow Lacey and Eleanora had managed to stay mounted during the frantic dash. Now, as the horses milled around inside the ruins, Eleanora sagged and started to slip from her horse. The ropes lashing her hands to the pommel of the saddle were all that held her up.

Helen Wayne suddenly appeared beside Eleanora's horse. She held one of the skinning knives in her hand, and it took only a second for her to slash the bindings. Helen caught Eleanora as she fell and then half carried, half dragged her over to Lacey's horse.

"Thanks," Lacey said as Helen cut her bonds. "Reckon there's no place for us to run now."

"I'm sorry, Lacey," Helen said. "I could kill that brother of mine for doing this to you."

"I intend to, if I ever get the chance."

Both of them knew Lacey meant the threat, and Helen did not blame the other woman. "Come on," she said. "Let's get over by the wagon."

Lacey helped her with Eleanora, and the three women reached the cover of the wagon and crouched there. The men defending the walls were firing as rapidly as they could, pouring lead into the charging Indians. Lacey risked a glance over the top of the

wagon and thought that the number of Indians seemed
to have diminished somewhat. She could not be sure of
that, given the dust and the confusion, and even if she
was right, she did not know what that might mean. She
ducked down as a bullet screamed through the air near
her head.

Burl Wayne now worked the lever of his Winchester, firing as fast as he could. He and his men were
taking a toll on the Indians, but there were still too
many of the Comanches. The Indian forces split and
circled, just as they had done back at the clump of
trees. Wayne jerked involuntarily as the man next to
him took an arrow in the throat and fell back in a
fountain of blood.

Another man fell, mortally wounded; then another.
From their position by the wagon, Lacey, Helen, and
Eleanora watched in horror as one of the hunters staggered toward them, his fingers clawing at the shaft of
the arrow in his chest. He lost his balance and fell
forward into the sand, the force of his fall driving the
arrow on through his body. Eleanora screamed as the
blood-smeared point ripped out through the man's back.

He had dropped his Winchester near his body, and
Lacey suddenly darted out from cover to scoop up the
rifle. She knelt next to the man for an instant to make
sure there was nothing she could do for him. He was
dead, beyond the help on anyone on earth.

Helen called, "Lacey, come back!" but Lacey ignored her. She ran to the wall and dropped to her
knees between two of the men. Throwing the rifle to
her shoulder, she aimed at the Comanches and started
triggering off shots as fast as she could work the Winchester's lever. As she fired, she glanced at the man to
her right and saw with a shock of recognition that it was
Ben Proctor.

Lacey felt a surge of anger. Proctor had betrayed
his passengers on the stage. But there was no time to
think about it now. They were united in their desperation as they faced the Indians.

The Comanches were closing their circle tighter
around the way station. Soon they would be leaping

their horses over the ruined walls and would be among
the hunters. Burl Wayne knew he and his men were
running low on ammunition, but that no longer mattered. Within a matter of minutes, there would be no
chance for reloading. It was over—except for the gruesome conclusion.

Proctor's rifle spat its last bullet. He threw it down
with a curse and stood up, yanking his revolver from its
holster. "Come and get it, you red sons of bitches!" he
howled, blasting away as several Comanches swerved
toward him. Two of the Indians were blown off their
horses by Proctor's shots, but another who carried a
lance urged his mount toward the crazed stage driver.
The tip of the lance drove into Proctor's body with a
solid *chunk*. He screamed as the force of the blow lifted
him off his feet for an instant. The Indian forced his
horse forward, right up to the wall.

Lacey fell over backward as Proctor's blood spattered her clothes. She tipped the barrel of her rifle up
and fired its final shot. The bullet caught the Indian
under his chin, flipping him off his horse with a stran-
gled grunt.

Lacey rolled over and sprang to her feet. She ran
back to the wagon, pausing for an instant to pick up a
Colt someone had dropped. She snapped open the
cylinder and saw that it still had three unfired bullets.
One for Helen, one for Eleanora . . . and one for herself. She might be willing to give up her own escape
into death, though, if she could get a clear shot at Burl
Wayne.

As she ran, her eyes scanned the feeble defenses at
the walls. Most of the hunters were down, either dead
or wounded. Only three or four were still on their feet
and fighting, and Wayne was not among them. Lacey
did not see his body on the ground, either.

Helen and Eleanora were still behind the wagon.
Both of them were unhurt so far, though several arrows
were stuck in the frame of the wagon itself. Eleanora
was on her knees, her mouth moving, and though Lacey
could not hear the words, she realized that Eleanora

was praying. Helen knelt at Eleanora's side, one of her hands on Eleanora's shoulder.

Lacey crouched behind Eleanora. Her eyes met Helen's, and she shook her head. There was no way out now, and both of them knew it.

When Lacey lifted the Colt in her hand, Helen nodded in resignation. Holding her breath, Lacey brought the barrel of the gun to a point just behind Eleanora's right ear.

It was better this way.

As the sound of shots came drifting through the air, Tucker McCall frowned and urged his borrowed horse on to more speed. He was riding at the front of the group of buffalo hunters, flanked by Bat Masterson and Billy Dixon. Allen Kerry and Willie Morse were close behind, along with the other hunters, all of whom had their rifles out and ready. Bringing up the rear was a small contingent looking after Rico Lopez and leading the horses bearing the bodies of Antonio Lopez and Louis Shepherd.

The group had been riding southwest for a couple of hours, looking for some sign of the party led by Burl Wayne. The distant shooting was the first such sign they had encountered, but it told a definite story to Tucker and the others.

"Reckon the Comanches caught up to them," Billy Dixon said. "We better hurry."

Tucker nodded grimly and leaned forward, willing the horse to go faster.

Within five minutes they had spotted the dust kicked up by the battle, and less than five minutes later they could see the Indians circling the ruins of what appeared to be an old way station. Some of the Comanches spotted them coming and broke away from the other warriors, whooping and racing their horses toward the newcomers.

Some of Masterson's men reined in and dropped out of their saddles to start firing at the Indians. The rest of the men continued riding hard toward the fight. Tucker was carrying his Sharps and was ready to use it, though the back of a galloping horse was not much of a firing platform. As he rode, the fear that had been festering in him all morning began to grow and threatened to take over his mind.

What if Lacey was already dead? He had been prepared never to see her again, but that was when he expected to die in the trees. Now he had been saved from that fate, but it would not mean a thing if he were too late to save the woman he loved. If she was still alive, the best thing he could do for her was to stay calm. He would stand a much better chance of rescuing her.

He forced the fear out of his head and let his eyes scan the bloody scene opening up in front of him.

He spotted the wagon and the stagecoach parked inside the ruins. There did not seem to be much opposition coming from inside the walls. One of the Comanches suddenly appeared in front of Tucker, swerving his horse toward him and lifting a Walker Colt stolen from some white man's body. Tucker did not want to waste the cartridge in the Sharps, so he thrust the barrel of the rifle out like a lance. The Indian's revolver blasted— almost in Tucker's face—and the slug clipped harmlessly past his head. Tucker's thrust went home, the barrel of the Sharps smacking into the Comanche's forehead with a dull thud. The Indian flew off his horse to land heavily and unmoving in the dirt.

There was hand-to-hand fighting all around Tucker now, as the Comanches responded to this new threat. Tucker's horse suddenly lurched beneath him, and he knew the animal had been hit. Kicking his feet out of the stirrups, he jumped free as the horse collapsed. After staggering a few steps, Tucker caught his balance and then looked up to see that he had ridden to within about a hundred yards of the ruins. He spotted the wagon again, through gaps in the fighting, and felt his heart leap as he recognized the flowing brunette hair of the woman crouched beside the vehicle.

Lacey was alive! With her were two other figures, probably Helen and Eleanora, and Lacey was holding a gun, slowly aiming it toward the head of one of the other women. Tucker was puzzled by the scene but was given no time to consider what might be happening.

One of the Indians left his horse in a leap that carried him over the walls. He came up with a knife clutched in his hand and ran toward the three women. Tucker's mouth went dry as he saw the warrior lunging at Lacey, who evidently did not hear him coming because of the uproar of battle.

Tucker did not think about it, letting his instincts take over instead. The Sharps came up, its butt smacking into his shoulder, and he aimed for barely an instant through the confusion. Then he pressed the trigger, and the Big Fifty roared.

The Indian screamed as the heavy slug punched through his body. He fell forward, already dead, and slammed into Lacey just as she pulled the trigger of the Colt. The pistol blasted, but the falling Indian had knocked her aim off. Eleanora shrieked and fell forward, clutching at her ear, the very tip of which had been grazed by Lacey's shot.

Lacey was stunned for a moment by the unexpectedness of the Indian crashing into her, but then she regained her senses and rolled out from under his corpse. Helen was kneeling by Eleanora, trying to see how seriously the older woman was hurt, and for a moment Lacey thought her shot had badly wounded the other woman. Then she saw that despite the blood, the injury was only a nick. She heard her name called and thought she was imagining things. The voice sounded like Tucker's—

He hurdled the wall and ran to her side, dropping his rifle and pulling her to her feet, folding her into his embrace. The fierceness of it drove the breath from her, but the breathlessness made her realize that she was not dreaming, that Tucker McCall really was here, holding her, protecting her. He had come, just as she had dreamed.

Long minutes passed, and neither of them knew it until they abruptly realized that the gunfire around them had drifted away. Tucker had his face buried in her hair, and when he lifted his gaze, he saw that the

Comanches were on the run again. They probably could not be sure how many buffalo hunters were firing at them, the devastatingly accurate rifle fire making it appear that the white men had a much larger force than they actually did.

One thing was certain. Tucker was never going to let Lacey go again.

And that was just fine with Lacey.

Allen Kerry rode into the ruins and hurriedly went to Eleanora's side. Helen was with her, trying to stop the bleeding from her ear with a piece of Eleanora's petticoat. "Is she all right?" Allen asked anxiously.

Helen nodded. "Reckon she will be, but she'll need to let a doctor tend to that ear. I'll bind it up as best I can."

Allen reached out and put his hand on Helen's arm. "What about you? Are you all right?"

She smiled. "Shoot, I'm fine. I never expected to see you and Tucker again, though."

"Another group of buffalo hunters came along just in time to help us out." Allen quickly explained about the hunters led by Bat Masterson and then tried to calm Eleanora. His soothing voice finally got through to her. A feeling of relief was strong in him, relief that they had reached here in time to save the women— relief that Helen Wayne in particular was all right.

He looked over Eleanora's shoulder and saw Tucker and Lacey embracing. There was none of the old jealousy in him as he said to Helen, "Those two look like they were meant to be together."

"Yes," Helen agreed, a touch of wistfulness in her voice. "Reckon Tucker found him the woman he always wanted."

The Indians had galloped out of sight by now, and the hunters were regrouping. Bat Masterson and Willie Morse rode into the ruins and looked over the carnage there. Willie grimaced as he spotted Ben Proctor's body skewered by the lance. No matter what he had done, Proctor deserved a better end than that.

All the other hunters from the original group were dead, Willie saw. The three women were the only survivors. Willie looked for one particular body and frowned when he did not see it. "That's funny," he told Masterson. "I don't see Burl Wayne here anywhere."

Across the ruins, Tucker was breaking the news about Antonio Lopez and Louis Shepherd to Lacey and Helen. Tears appeared in their eyes when they thought about Rico Lopez, orphaned now. Eleanora was the only one who had really liked Shepherd, but they sympathized with his death, too.

Willie Morse came up to Tucker a moment later and said in a low voice, "Wayne's not here, Mr. McCall."

Tucker frowned. "He's got to be."

"Well, he's not," Willie said, shaking his head. "I've checked all the bodies."

Tucker turned to Lacey and Helen. "Did either of you see what happened to Wayne?"

"There was too much confusion," Lacey replied. "I saw Ben Proctor killed, but he was the only one I knew. There were Indians everywhere, and dust and gun smoke."

"I didn't see him, either," Helen put in. She felt a curious emptiness when she thought of her adopted brother. She was not mourning his almost-certain death. She was not feeling much of anything.

"I guess he could have slipped off somehow during the fighting. Doesn't seem likely he could have gotten very far, though."

Billy Dixon had ridden up while Tucker was talking, and without dismounting, he said, "Don't know who you're talkin' about, McCall, but we ain't got time to look for his body." He turned his gaze to Masterson. "We'd best get out of here, Bat. I don't think ol' Quanah's likely to come back for more today, but you never know."

"I agree with Billy," Masterson told Tucker and the others. "We'll all head back to Adobe Walls. You'll be safe enough there. It's only a couple of hours farther south."

A couple of hours . . . Burl Wayne's mad dash had almost paid off.

Her ear bandaged rudely but effectively, Eleanora

was made comfortable in the bed of the wagon on the hides. Helen climbed onto the seat to take the reins, and Allen joined her there. "I've had enough of sitting in a saddle," he said with a grin. "Lacey, why don't you take my horse?"

"All right," Lacey nodded. "Oh, Tucker, there's Rico."

The men in charge of Rico and the two dead men were riding up to the ruins, and Lacey hurried to the boy. The two of them had become close during this ordeal, and he went into her arms in a rush. Tucker watched as she tenderly talked to Rico, assuring him that she would look after him. Once again Tucker thought what a remarkable lady she was.

When everyone was mounted up again and Willie Morse was on the box of the stagecoach to handle the team, Bat Masterson waved his hand and called, "Let's move out, folks!" The group got under way, leaving behind them the ruins littered with the bodies of white men and Comanche alike. There was no time to do anything else, not if the ones still living were going to be saved.

Tucker glanced back once. It was a grim sight, one that none of them would ever forget.

Three hundred yards away, crouched just beneath the lip of a little gully, Burl Wayne watched them ride away. His breathing was harsh, and his buckskin shirt was plastered to his side with blood that had already dried. He had taken an arrow in the side, and the point of it was still there, though he had broken off the shaft.

The fight in the ruins was like a bad dream to him. He was not sure how he had gotten out here; all he remembered was falling when the arrow hit him and then getting up and running, dodging between horses and men, coughing as he sucked down the lungfuls of dust. Then suddenly the battle had been behind him, and he had flopped on his belly in the sparse brush, crawling away from there.

Now the fighting was over. Wayne did not know who the newcomers were, but he recognized Tucker

McCall's tall figure among them. He saw the wagon and the stage roll out of the ruins and start south, guarded by the large band of men.

They were leaving him out here, leaving him to die. And they were taking the hides—*his hides*—with them!

Goddamn thieves, that was what they were. He heaved himself to his feet and winced as pain shot through his body. They could not get away with stealing from him. He had worked too damned hard for those hides. Nobody was going to take those hides from him. Nobody!

Wayne blinked his eyes, unaware of what the pain and the blood loss and the heat were doing to his mind. He slipped his knife out of its sheath and looked down at the blade. It caught the sunlight and flashed in his eyes, blurring his vision even more.

He would kill them, kill the goddamn thieves! Teach them to steal from Burl Wayne, dammit!

Slowly, the wound in his side burning, Burl Wayne began to plod toward the way station. There were still horses there, horses that had belonged to dead men. He would catch one of them or die trying.

He was going to Adobe Walls.

Chapter Eleven

Adobe Walls had begun its existence as a trading post and way station. Ten years earlier, in 1864, it had been the scene of a battle between the Comanches and a group of white men led by Kit Carson. The Walls, as it was called, had been abandoned after that, until recently, when a small village had sprung up near the original site. The buildings had thick sod walls and roofs and were lined up in a row facing east. There was a trading post, a saloon, a smithy, a restaurant, and a rude hotel. It was a little touch of civilization in the middle of a trackless wilderness.

To the weary riders who arrived there late that afternoon, it looked like heaven.

It helped that a cavalry patrol was stopping there. The arrival of Masterson's party swelled the number of hunters in Adobe Walls to over a hundred; the presence of the soldiers added to that made it fairly certain that the Comanches would not risk an attack on the town.

As the group came to a halt in front of Leonard and Rath's Trading Post, Bat Masterson said to Tucker, "You better come with me, McCall. I'm going to talk to the officer in command of that patrol. He'll want to know what happened to you people."

Tucker nodded and then looked over at Lacey, who was riding beside him. "You'll be all right?" he asked.

"Of course. We'll get Eleanora settled in the hotel and find a doctor to look at her ear."

Tucker and Masterson dismounted and walked into the trading post to look for the cavalry officer while Lacey and Allen got Eleanora out of the wagon and helped her into the hotel. She was long past protesting the crude accommodations.

After finding the officer and filling him in on the movements of the Indians, Tucker stepped back out into the street and looked up at the sky. The sun was down now, and the sky was fading to a deep, dark blue. Stars seemed to wink into existence as Tucker stood there with the evening breeze in his face. It was good to be alive.

He strolled down to the hotel to find Lacey and the others. As he passed by the saloon, he heard the off-key tinkling of a piano, the laughter of men, the clink of bottles against glasses, and for a moment he was tempted to stop. But he shook his head with a wry grin. He could have used a drink, all right, but he wanted to be back with Lacey even more.

The proprietor of the hotel told him that Lacey, Allen, and Helen had gone over to the restaurant. Tucker thanked him and then went to the restaurant, ducking as he entered so that his tall frame would clear the low doorway.

Several lanterns gave the place a warm glow. He saw his three companions seated at one of the tables enjoying a hot meal, and his mouth began to water as succulent aromas drifted in from the kitchen.

Lacey greeted him with a smile. "Did you find that cavalry officer?" she asked.

"Yes," Tucker replied as he pulled out a chair and sat down next to her. He looked across the table at Allen. "How's your sister?"

"I think she'll be all right," he said. "There's no doctor here, but one of the troopers has had some medical training. He cleaned the wound and bandaged it. We'll get proper treatment for it on down the line."

"Is the stage going on?"

Allen nodded. "Willie talked to the troop's sergeant. They're heading south, and they've agreed to accompany the coach."

Tucker nodded. "Their lieutenant said something about that while Masterson and I were talking to him." Another thought occurred to him. "What about that little shaver?"

Lacey smiled. "Rico is going to visit my father's ranch with me, but then he's going on to San Antonio to live with his relatives. He says that was his father's plan, and he wants to follow through with it. I told him he'll have a place on the ranch with me any time he wants it, though."

Tucker smiled at her words while the proprietor's wife, an attractive woman named Nancy Olds, came to the table bearing a platter of food for him. She had not taken an order from him, since the fare here was simple and limited. It did not matter to Tucker. The big plate full of steak, beans, and potatoes looked mighty appealing to him. Before he dug in, though, he had to have the answer to a question.

"Are you staying in Texas?" he asked Lacey.

She met his gaze and nodded. "I may go back to visit my mother from time to time, but I can't fight it any longer. This is my home down here, and I'm staying."

"After all that's happened, most people would say you've lost your mind," Allen said.

"Maybe so," Lacey replied, obviously not caring at all what most people might think.

Tucker nodded thoughtfully. "I'd like to see that ranch of your father's," he said.

"I thought you might."

Helen spoke up. "Lacey staying in Texas is a fair exchange, Tucker. I'm going to Boston."

Tucker glanced at Allen Kerry in surprise and saw that the young man seemed to be blushing. But the light was not too good in here; he could have been mistaken, he thought with a slight smile.

"Is that so? Well, I reckon I'm glad for you, Helen. What are you planning on doing back there?"

"Allen's gonna help me go to school and get some learning."

"An education, Helen. I'm going to help you get an education," Allen said gently.

Tucker and Lacey glanced at each other. It looked like a definite friendship had sprung up between Allen and Helen. Whether it would develop into anything more was hard to say, but the seeds were there.

Lacey had to hide a grin. One thing was certain: Helen would make quite an impression on Allen's family. Lacey wished she could be there to see that.

But she would not trade it for staying here in Texas . . . with Tucker McCall.

A new voice spoke up. "Did I hear you say you were going back east, Miss Helen?" Willie Morse asked. He had entered the restaurant with the cavalry lieutenant and Bat Masterson.

"That's right," Helen said. "Allen's gonna pay my way."

"Reckon you can pay your own way, ma'am," Masterson said. "You're a rich lady."

Helen frowned in confusion. "I don't know what you're talking about."

"We just unloaded all those buffalo hides down at the trading post," Willie said. "Mr. Masterson and Lieutenant Schutz here agree that they belong to you."

Helen stared at them. "The hides . . ."

"Mr. Rath has made a generous offer on them," Masterson told her. "And since your brother is dead . . ." He shrugged.

Helen looked around the table and shook her head. "I don't want the money," she said. "God, look how many people got killed over them damn hides."

"That's one reason you should take it," Tucker told her firmly. "What Burl did wasn't your fault, Helen, and you shouldn't have to suffer anymore for it."

Helen thought it over and nodded after a moment. "All right. I won't take all of it, though. You were part of the original group, Tucker. You deserve some of the money." She held up a hand to forestall the protest that Tucker started to make. "In fact, I think all of us who came through it should have a share. What do you think, Willie?"

Willie looked surprised. He said, "That's mighty generous of you, Miss Helen, but you don't have to—"

"I know I don't have to. I want to."

Willie grinned. "In that case, I reckon I like the idea just fine, ma'am."

Helen turned to the others. "Allen? Lacey? How about it?"

"Neither one of us needs the money," Lacey said. "But I'm perfectly willing to take a share . . . and give it to Rico Lopez."

"Yes," Allen nodded. "That's a good idea. And I'm sure Eleanora will feel the same way," Allen added. He turned in his seat and called Nancy Olds over to the table. "Mrs. Olds, I suppose it would be too much to ask for you to have some champagne around here?"

Nancy Olds grinned. "We don't have any champagne, but how about some elderberry wine my husband's grandma made up back home?"

"Bring it on, dear lady, bring it on."

Homemade wine in battered tin cups had never tasted so good as when they all raised their drinks and Allen Kerry said, "To survival."

"Amen to that," Bat Masterson added.

Outside, in the shadows near the door, there was movement as a figure leaned close to the opening and listened to what was being said inside. The shadowy figure supported itself against the wall for a moment and then scuttled back into the deeper darkness as Lieutenant Schutz said, "I'd best be going."

"I'll go with you, Lieutenant," Masterson said, and Willie Morse echoed him.

The three men went out of the restaurant, leaving Lacey, Tucker, Allen, and Helen at the table. Tucker dug into his food with enthusiasm while the others finished up their meals. By the time the last bit of gravy on his plate was cleaned up, the effects of the last few days were starting to set in. No sleep, desperate fighting, and the clout on the head all combined to make Tucker think longingly of a nice soft bed. It had been a hell of a long time since he had slept in a bed.

He listened as Lacey and Allen and Helen made their plans. Allen was not going on to Sam Ellis's ranch with Lacey. He and Helen and Eleanora would go along on the stage until it reached a station where they could catch one heading east. They planned to return to Boston as soon as possible.

Allen reached across the table and let his hand rest briefly on Helen's. "You're going to set Boston on its ear, my dear," he told her.

Tucker had pulled out a pipe and was packing it when Allen asked him, "What about you, Tucker? What does the future hold for you?"

Tucker mused for a moment before answering, "Appears to me like the day of the buffalo hunter is about over. Two or three years more and the herds will all be gone. Reckon it's about time to try my hand at something else."

"Cattle ranching, maybe?" Lacey asked.

Tucker nodded. "Might be nice to help something grow, instead of helping to kill it off."

A few minutes later, Allen and Helen stood up. "It seems to be a nice night," he said. "I believe we'll take a walk and sample the night air."

Tucker and Lacey nodded their good-nights and watched as Allen and Helen strolled out the door of the restaurant. "Seems like a strange team to be pulling in double harness," Tucker commented.

"Sometimes that works the best," Lacey said.

He could not argue with that.

The storms of the last few days seemed to be gone now. The night sky was clear and swimming with stars and moonlight as Allen and Helen stepped outside. He took a deep breath and slipped his arm through hers. She did not seem to mind; indeed, she had a happy smile on her face as she fell into step beside him.

They had gone only a few feet when a shape darted from the shadows at the corner of the building. Helen had time only to say, "What—" before she felt a sudden fiery pain in her side. She stumbled, pressing her hand to her body and feeling hot wetness as an insane laugh split the night.

"Allen . . ." she said weakly and then sagged against him.

"Steal my hides, will you! I'll teach you, you whore!" Burl Wayne screamed as he danced around in front of the stunned pair brandishing his bloody knife. "I followed you. You thought I was dead. You thought you could steal my hides! I'll kill you!" He lunged at Allen, slashing at him with the blade.

Tucker and Lacey heard the commotion outside. Tucker recognized Wayne's voice and came to his feet, moving with a speed he would not have thought possible in his exhausted condition. He was out the door in an instant, clutching the Sharps that he had been carrying with him for so long it felt like part of his arm. Lacey was right behind him.

Tucker's eyes, accustomed to the light inside, could not tell what was happening at first. But then he saw Burl Wayne leaping at Allen and saw moonlight glint off the knife clutched in Wayne's fist. Tucker leaped forward, thrusting out the barrel of the rifle, and Wayne's blade deflected off it with a clang. Tucker surged ahead, swinging his left arm in a looping backhand that caught Wayne on the jaw and sent him reeling—but did not cause Wayne to drop the knife.

"Get back!" Tucker snapped at Allen. Allen had his arms around Helen, supporting her, and he half carried her back to the entrance of the restaurant where Lacey was waiting.

"You just hold it right there, Wayne!" Tucker yelled at the crazed little buffalo hunter, covering him with the Sharps.

"You thought I was dead, didn't you, you bastard!" Wayne shrieked back at him. "You're in on it! I heard you! You're all plannin' to steal my hides!"

The uproar was rousing the whole village. Bat Masterson, Billy Dixon, Willie Morse, and the cavalry lieutenant came running to see what was going on. Several people stepped out of the buildings carrying lanterns, and the glow from them lit up the street and showed the filthy, bloody creature that had been Burl Wayne.

"Back off, Wayne," Tucker said softly. "We don't want any more trouble with you."

Wayne's only response was to howl, "I'll kill you!"

"Helen's all right, Tucker," Lacey called to him. She and Allen were kneeling beside Helen, and they had been joined by the trooper who had cared for Eleanora's injury. Lacey went on, "He's just cut her side. It's bleeding a lot, but she's not in danger!"

Lieutenant Schutz stepped forward and raised his voice. "Put down that knife, Mr. Wayne. I'm placing you under arrest for what you've done to these people the last few days. It'll go easier for you if you come quietly."

Wayne ignored him and stared slit-eyed at Tucker. "All your fault," he muttered. "All your fault, McCall . . . *Aaaaaaaahhhh!*" He raised the knife and leaped at Tucker, screaming out his hate.

"Damn," Tucker said. He raised the Big Fifty and fired.

The slug punched a hole the size of a fist through Burl Wayne, knocking him off his feet. Tucker looked at the body lying in the street and shook his head. He heard the lieutenant and Bat Masterson agreeing behind him that it was a clear case of self-defense. Tucker did not really care about that. He had just done what needed to be done.

He turned and saw Helen being carried into the hotel by several of the troopers. Allen was beside her, holding her hand and talking to her. There was a smile on Helen's face. Troopers hurried past Tucker going out into the street to tend to Burl Wayne's body. Tucker barely saw them.

Lacey stood in the light spilling from the restaurant doorway. He began walking toward her, and she came forward into his arms. Both of them knew that the long nightmare was finally over, for good this time.

"We can go home now," Lacey whispered, back to the ranch where her heart had always been.

"Home," he repeated, and the word sounded right on his lips.

Home. Lacey was returning to hers, and Tucker had finally found his.

Author's Note

A few months later, early on the morning of Saturday, June 27, 1874, the village of Adobe Walls was awakened by a loud cracking noise. One of the ridgepoles in the roof of Hanrahan's Saloon had split, and it turned out to be a very fortunate accident. On that morning, a large force of Indians—Comanches, Kiowas, Cheyenne, and Arapaho—numbering at least five hundred and led by Chief Quanah, attacked the trading post. Instead of finding the hunters asleep and easy prey, however, the Indians found them awake and ready to fight, and what had been planned as a massacre turned into a five-day siege. The hunters with their buffalo rifles took a deadly toll before the Indians finally gave up and left. It was reported that Billy Dixon shot Quanah's horse out from under him at a distance of just over a mile. Bat Masterson also took part in the Battle of Adobe Walls before going on to an illustrious career as gunfighter, gambler, lawman, and journalist. Quanah later took the name of his white mother and became Quanah Parker, one of the great chiefs of the Comanche nation who helped bring about peace between the white man and the Indians.

By 1878, the buffalo were gone.